One Clear, Ice-Cold
January Morning at
the Beginning of the
Twenty-First Century

ROLAND
SCHIMMELPFENNIG

One Clear, Ice-Cold January Morning at the Beginning of the Twenty-First Century

*Translated from the German by
Jamie Bulloch*

MACLEHOSE PRESS
QUERCUS · LONDON

First published in the German language as
An einem klaren, eiskalten Januarmorgen zu Beginn des 21. Jahrhunderts
by S. Fischer Verlag in 2016

First published in Great Britain in 2018 by MacLehose Press
This paperback edition published in 2019 by

MacLehose Press
An imprint of Quercus Publishing Ltd
Carmelite House
50 Victoria Embankment
London EC4Y 0DZ

An Hachette UK company

The translation of this work was supported by a grant from the Goethe-Institut.

ISBN (MMP) 978 0 85705 697 9
ISBN (Ebook) 978 0 85705 696 2

10 9 8 7 6 5 4 3 2 1

Designed and typeset in Scala by Libanus Press
Printed and bound in Great Britain by Clays Ltd, Elcograf S.p.A.

One clear, ice-cold January morning at the beginning of the twenty-first century, just after daybreak, a solitary wolf crossed the frozen river marking the border between Germany and Poland.

The wolf came from the east. He trotted across the ice of the frozen Oder to the other bank, then kept heading westwards. Behind the river the sun stood low over the horizon.

Beneath a cloudless sky the wolf wandered in the morning light across the expanses of snow-covered fields until he came to the edge of a forest and vanished into it.

The following day, thirty kilometres to the west of the frozen river, a hunter found the remains of a deer in the woods. In the snow beside the dead deer the hunter discovered the tracks of a wolf.

This was near Vierlinden bei Seelow. No wolf had been seen there for more than one hundred and sixty years, not since 1843.

The wolf remained in this area until mid-February. Nobody actually saw the creature, they only found his tracks and bloody prey in the snow.

The winter was very cold and very long. Towards the end of the second week in February the snow came and continued uninterruptedly for several days.

On the evening of February 16 a fuel tanker spun out of control on the motorway between Poland and Berlin, which was completely covered in snow.

The tanker jack-knifed and toppled onto its side. Two other lorries crashed into it and caught fire. The fuel tanker exploded. Not one of the drivers survived.

In the wake of this collision sixty vehicles skidded into each other on the slippery carriageway and were jammed together. People were unable to get out of their crushed cars and the fire continued to spread.

The accident happened close to Glieningmoor. A more than forty-kilometre tailback soon built up, stretching all the way to the Polish border. The motorway was closed in both directions.

Night fell. The drivers of the vehicles in the tailback turned off their engines and headlights. Snow settled on the motorway in the darkness and on the stationary cars.

Fire engines and ambulances drove up the hard shoulder past the never-ending columns of vehicles. It kept snowing. Nothing was moving.

The young Polish man was on his way to Berlin from a village near Warsaw and had been driving for eleven hours. For the last three he had been stationary on the motorway in snow. In the distance he could see the glow of the vehicles still on fire.

The exploded fuel tanker and the jumble of smashed-up vehicles lay about three kilometres ahead of him.

The engine of his old Toyota was switched off. The young man was freezing. He didn't have enough petrol to keep the engine running. Occasionally he turned the key halfway to start up the windscreen wipers for a few seconds. He was worried about the battery. He left the internal light off and didn't turn on the radio. He sat in the Toyota in darkness.

This is going to take another twenty hours, he'd heard a Polish lorry driver shout earlier on the carriageway. This is going to take another twenty hours, the man had shouted over and over again.

Grabbing his mobile, the young Pole got out of his car and took some photos of the distant glow from the fire in the night. Then he got back into the car. The pictures were too fuzzy to make out anything.

He called his girlfriend, Agnieszka, who was waiting for him in Berlin.

"No, this is going to take hours yet."

"What are you doing?" she said. "Have you got a blanket?"

"I've got the sleeping bag in the boot."

"Leave the car there and walk to the nearest village."

"There aren't any villages here."

"There's always a village somewhere. There must be one."

"There's nothing here. I can't see a thing."

"There must be a village, Tomasz. Walk to the nearest village; you'll freeze to death there."

"There's no village here. And I can't just abandon the car."

After another hour in the tailback without moving, Tomasz got out of the car to wander up to the scene of the accident. Before he set off he looked for a marker, as he knew that he wouldn't find the snowed-in Toyota again unless he had some sort of orientation point.

By the side of the motorway to his right was a sign that read BERLIN 80 KM.

I'm a boy scout, he thought, I'm a fucking boy scout.

Tomasz made his way to the scene of the accident. The snow continued to fall. The blue lights of the emergency vehicles spun in the darkness. As he got closer he could see the blue-and-white flames of the blowtorches the firemen were using to try to free passengers from the mangled vehicles. He could hear shouting and screaming. A man of about sixty stood by the side of the motorway in the thick snow flurries. A muscular type, he wore a bloodied vest. Probably a long-distance lorry driver.

"Is there anything I can do to help?" Tomasz called out to the man in Polish. He thought he recognised him from Warsaw, but the man called back:

"Look after your own shit."

A helicopter landed on the other side of the motorway. Floodlights had been set up. Paramedics carried someone on a stretcher to one of the ambulances, going as fast as they could. A woman ran beside the stretcher. She kept shouting something, a word, a name perhaps, then she slipped and fell in the snow. The paramedics ran on.

Tomasz turned and headed back into the darkness between the stationary cars.

Three emergency vehicles with blue lights drove along the hard shoulder towards the scene of the accident. In the deep snow he looked for his marker, the sign with the distance to Berlin. He found his snow-covered Toyota and fetched the sleeping bag from the boot.

Tomasz had been living in Berlin with Agnieszka for three years. Mostly he worked for Marek, another Pole. Marek and his team gutted houses or renovated them. They could do everything.

In Poland Tomasz had always worked alone. When he'd found work outside Warsaw he would sometimes spend the night in a sleeping bag on building sites or in the car – but he couldn't do that in Germany.

Ever since moving to Germany Tomasz had no longer been able to work alone. Since moving to Germany he could no longer be alone.

*

The lock on the Toyota's boot was frozen. To his right stood the sign: eighty kilometres to Berlin.

Then he saw the wolf. The wolf was standing in front of the sign at the side of the snowy motorway, seven metres in front of him, no more.

A wolf, Tomasz thought, that looks like a wolf, it's probably a large dog, who would let their dog roam around here, or is it really a wolf?

He took a photograph of the animal in front of the sign in the driving snow. The flash in the darkness.

A moment later the wolf had vanished.

She had a bruise beneath her right eye and a split lip.

The girl was sitting under the shelter of the only bus stop in the village. The village was called Sauen, near Beeskow, in the Oder-Spree district.

It was early in the morning, half past six. Still dark. She was waiting for the school bus. She was sixteen. The evening before, her mother had punched her twice in the face.

The snow fell in the cone of light from the streetlamp. The village consisted of no more than a few houses along a country road.

Sitting beside her on the bench beneath the shelter of the bus stop was her boyfriend.

"Let's get away from here," she said to her boyfriend.

The two of them were wearing heavy leather jackets, combat boots, chains, earrings, but they had soft faces and light bodies.

"Where do you want to go?" he said.

"Berlin," she said.

By the time the bus arrived they had already left. They didn't walk along the road. On the road sooner or later someone would have stopped them – two children out in the snow in the early morning. They went cross-country.

The girl was called Elisabeth and the boy Micha.

When they got to the forest it stopped snowing for the first time in four days.

"Fuck, fuck, fuck," Charly said, smiling and opening his eyes wide. "Look at that, look at that!"

Jacky followed his gaze out of the window onto the street, but there was nothing there, nothing out of the ordinary. Cars, passers-by. It had stopped snowing.

"Other people used to live here, it used to be different here."

"Charly, you haven't got a clue who used to live here."

"But surely you can see it, surely you can."

"We didn't use to live here."

"Nor do we live here now."

"Of course we live here."

"We don't live *here*. Here."

Berlin, Prenzlauer Berg. Prior to 1989 the shop had been a bakery. After the wall came down one of the old shop assistants had taken over the bakery and, with very little money, had turned it into a kiosk, a so-called convenience shop. She kept two rabbits in a cage behind the counter, but then got into trouble with the authorities and the rabbits had to go. She used to stay open until late, selling newspapers, cigarettes, beer, schnapps, crisps and coke, and if the old people who lived nearby couldn't make it to her kiosk she would go up to their apartments with newspapers, beer and cigarettes, but that was over now. The shop didn't earn enough, the rents increased and she gave it up at the age of sixty-five. Then Charly and Jacky, young people, came to take over the shop. They had saved up and had been looking for something just like it. They repainted the walls: black, gold and dark red.

"You're making such a funny face, do you know that, Charly? Such a funny face, your eyes are like saucers. What's the matter with you?"

"Do you know, that's just what I was going to say to you, love? You look strange, you have done all day, what is it, what are you thinking?"

"I'm thinking that something's not quite right, but I can't put my finger on it."

"I can tell you what's not right: there aren't enough people. I mean, the shop's ticking over alright, but still there aren't enough people coming through the door."

"That's because of the weather, Charly."

"And then you pull a funny face and tell me *I'm* making a funny face." Charly opened his eyes wide again.

"Do you think we'll ever have children?"

"Of course, of course we will, but don't you think it's a bit soon. I mean, we've only just opened the shop, shouldn't we settle down a bit here first? You're twenty-nine . . ."

"I'm almost thirty, and you've hardly got any hair left."

"We've still got loads of time."

But she knew that this wasn't the case. She sensed she would never have children.

"O.K., fine," Charly said. "Fine, what if . . . what if, let's think it all through properly first, from start to finish." His eyes were like saucers again. "From start to finish, fuck."

The man had made himself a thermos of coffee and some sandwiches. He took the binoculars and rifle, his hunting gun, but no dog. The dog had died before Christmas. The old man hadn't told anyone that he would be going to the woods before daybreak. He put on warm clothes, his boots, long coat and hat, and as he crossed the yard he whistled for his dog, but the dog didn't come and then he remembered that he no longer had a dog.

The snow was deep and the man made slow progress along the forest path. He'd been going for almost an hour and a half when he reached the raised hide just before dawn. He had not come to shoot anything. He was only here because he loved this place, the raised hide, the dawn, the field before him, the edge of the woods on the other side. The man often came here early in the morning, even in winter.

He'd heard that a wolf had been sighted in the vicinity of Seelow, north of here. He knew that wolves roamed. Wolves lived in packs, but some animals had to leave the pack and then they roamed to find a new one. They could cover great distances, sometimes seventy kilometres or more in a day.

The man sat up in his hide just before dawn, gazing out at the snowy field. He sipped coffee from the thermos. His wife had never liked it when he went to the woods alone, out of concern for him and also out of concern for herself or insecurity. She had never liked him going off with the dog and leaving her behind.

The man had not come to shoot anything, he could have left his rifle at home.

It became light. On this morning the man saw no game, no deer, no wild boar. He thought he'd glimpsed a movement at the edge of the forest on the far side of the field, but he couldn't see anything through his binoculars.

All of a sudden he felt unwell, he felt sick, his palms were sweaty, his heart thumping. Death is coming for me, he thought, this is it.

He felt better again after a few minutes, although he was bathed in sweat and knew he had to get back. He was worried he wouldn't make it.

In the end it had taken Tomasz seventeen hours to get from Warsaw to Berlin. He'd set off in the late morning of February 16. That evening a fuel tanker had skidded on the motorway forty kilometres beyond the Polish border. The tanker had jack-knifed, overturned, caught fire and finally exploded. More than sixty vehicles had braked and smashed into each other. It had taken eight hours to clear the motorway. Tomasz had sat stationary until three o'clock in the morning – ahead of him the glow of the fire in the darkness, later the floodlights.

He had seen a wolf not ten metres away, a wolf on the hard shoulder.

"You saw . . . what did you see? A wolf?" Agnieszka laughed. "You're going crazy, darling."

He had just arrived and was sitting opposite her in the small kitchen of their apartment in Neukölln. It was four o'clock in the morning, perhaps a little later. There was virtually nothing to eat at home, just tea and beer.

"I bought you some beer."

"Haven't you got any soup? It was so cold in the car, I think I'm getting ill."

"You didn't really see a wolf . . ."

"I sat for eight hours in the freezing Toyota."

"Where did you see this wolf?"

They had a cheap one-bedroom apartment from the 1960s. It had low ceilings and was dark and noisy. The walls were thin. A neon tube shone from the ceiling of the tiny kitchen.

"Are you going straight to the site?"

"Yes," he said.

"I see. I thought you were getting ill."

"On the hard shoulder. I saw it on the hard shoulder."

She laughed. Agnieszka was twenty-two. She and Tomasz had been together since she was fourteen. He was two years older. They came from the same village, not far from Warsaw. They'd been living in Berlin for three years.

She cleaned shops, businesses, open-plan offices, she cleaned for artists, film people, journalists and sometimes she looked after their children. She'd fallen into these circles by chance and then kept getting recommended. When she and Tomasz arrived in Berlin, neither of them had spoken German. Now Agnieszka spoke almost flawless German while he still understood practically nothing. On the building sites he worked almost exclusively with other Poles.

"At the side of the road. On the hard shoulder."

The two of them worked a lot, as much as possible, day

and night. They didn't sleep much. When he finished on the building site he came and helped her clean, at night on the deserted office floors at Rosa-Luxemburg-Platz or in Schönhauserallee.

They worked from six or seven in the morning until late at night, from Monday to Saturday afternoon. On Saturday night they would go dancing.

"I took a photo."

She looked at the picture.

"You photographed a wolf?"

"That's what I'm telling you."

"Do you think many people took photos of the wolf?"

"No. Nobody."

"A wolf on the motorway," she said. "In the snow."

"In the traffic jam. A wolf in the traffic jam."

She laughed. That had been meant as a joke. He rarely told jokes. Hardly ever.

They hadn't seen each other for almost four weeks; he had been doing some work for a relative near Warsaw. She looked at him. They'd known each other since they were children and had been together for eight years. They'd come to Berlin together, unmarried.

In the eyes of their Catholic relatives they were living in sin. Back then they'd driven to Berlin in the Toyota, and had found the apartment in Neukölln through friends.

They survived on crisps and coke and biscuits and tea and

beer, because they didn't like the food in Germany and because they had no time to cook.

They were always cheerful, they could always keep going. Nothing can flatten me, she would joke, and now, as she saw him sitting at the kitchen table, she realised that he couldn't keep going. She saw that the strength was slowly seeping out of him. He had been getting quieter and quieter for months. He'd begun to spend weeks on end in Poland because a distant relative there had work for him.

"Tomek, have you thought about selling the picture?"

"The picture? Which picture?"

"The photo. The photo of the wolf."

"Who would I sell it to? Who's going to buy it off me?"

The bus driver had stopped, and when he didn't see the girl and the boy he waited for a moment, at just after half past six in the morning at the only bus stop in the village. He waited longer than he ought to, he was late anyway because of the snow, and he knew the children, they got on his bus every morning, and he knew the boy's mother, he had once been married to her sister, a long, long time ago.

Later that morning he'd called the boy's mother and asked her whether everything was alright, that's what you do in the country.

They'd hardly slept, Agnieszka and Tomasz, no more than an hour. They had lain in bed without touching each other, even though they hadn't seen each other for almost four weeks, and then the alarm went off.

A few hours later Agnieszka showed the photograph to a woman whose house she cleaned. The woman worked for a newspaper. She bought the photograph from Agnieszka and the following day it was everywhere: a wolf in the snow at night, in the light of a flash, and behind the wolf a sign – eighty kilo-metres to Berlin.

In spite of the deep snow the boy and girl were fast, too fast, at least for the first few hours. At half past six in the morning they'd set off from the bus stop in the dark. At ten o'clock that morning the village was already twenty kilometres behind them. They were a long way into the woods. They were freezing and sweating, they were hungry and most of all they were thirsty. They ate snow. They both knew that they wouldn't get far, but they kept going all the same.

In the forest it was almost completely silent. It was a grey day. The boy and girl didn't speak much. They walked beside each other without exchanging a word and sometimes they stopped in the snow to roll cigarettes as best they could in the cold with stiff fingers, and smoked. The smoking helped against the hunger.

They walked through the woods without seeing another soul. At a fork in the forest path stood an old construction trailer. The door was open. Inside the trailer were heaps of rubbish, empty cigarette packets, brochures, old newspapers, empty beer bottles, cigarette butts. There had been a fire in the trailer at some point. In one corner was a stove, a small wood stove.

They came across the trailer in the early afternoon. They didn't dare light a fire in the stove as they were worried that the trailer might burn down.

They collected wood and tried to make a fire outside, but for a long while had no success. By the time they had a fire burning beside the trailer it was dark. They knew it was too cold to sleep outside in the snow, even next to the fire. They could survive the night inside the trailer, but only if they could get the stove to burn without the entire vehicle going up in flames. They lit a fire in the stove and waited. The trailer didn't go up in flames. It soon warmed up in the small space. After hours in the snow the two of them quickly grew tired in the warmth, despite their hunger. Outside, their camp fire glowed in the dark.

In the distance they could hear a rushing noise.

"That might be the motorway," he said. "Or the main road."

The boy and girl huddled on the floor of the trailer beside the stove. They leaned against each other, trying not to fall asleep because they were still afraid that the trailer might catch fire and burn down, but their eyes kept closing.

The girl's mother did nothing. It wasn't the first time the girl had failed to come home.

But that evening a woman from the police was at her front door and then the missing person's announcement was issued.

Yes, she and her daughter had quarrelled.

The policewoman was also from the village. She knew the two children, she knew the boy's family and she knew the girl's mother too.

About fifteen years ago, the girl's mother, or to be more precise, her then husband, had bought the empty schoolhouse in the village for not very much money, and she used to come here from Berlin for weekends with her husband and daughter.

They knew the couple from the newspapers, from television. The man was older, a successful painter. Later, when the girl was around three, the man stopped coming.

After separating from her husband the girl's mother no longer received any commissions, or too few. She gave up her apartment in Berlin and moved into the village schoolhouse with her daughter. She was a celebrity, with dyed-red hair and loose-fitting trousers when she wasn't working in her overalls in the schoolyard or in her workshop.

She was in her early thirties when she had the child, and a successful artist in Berlin. Five years later she was living as a single mother in a village not far from the Polish border. She drank too much, she always had, and was an irascible and self-righteous woman. She had fallen out with most of the people from her time in Berlin.

She told her daughter that she'd moved out of Berlin because of her. So that she, the daughter, could have a better childhood than the one she'd had herself, a different childhood from one spent in a tenement block on the north-eastern fringe of Berlin, capital city of the G.D.R.

But the reasons changed depending on how much she had drunk. Sometimes she might tell the child that she'd had to move out of Berlin as a single mother because she couldn't afford her studio space in the city anymore.

There was the version in which the city had no more to offer after her daughter's birth and Berlin had lost any artistic significance overnight, the parties, the scene, and there was the version in which she'd stopped working during her pregnancy and after the birth for the sake of her child – because of the noise when she used the chainsaw or the chisel – and the market had never forgiven her this enforced break.

When the few remaining friends came to visit, the child might hear other versions. Occasionally there was talk of important commissions that had been withdrawn due to intriguing by her ex-husband, and sometimes she would say that she was suffering from a crisis, she'd had artist's block since the birth.

She barely worked. But there was always something to do and it was always important: the garden, the house.

Whenever she left the house she would dress as if a city crowd were waiting outside in the village street.

Even when the girl was little the mother had kept predicting to the daughter that one day she would hate her mother as much as the woman had hated her own mother.

When the girl was eleven the woman realised that her prediction had been correct. That the day had arrived. She had always shouted and sometimes she hit the child. Not often, not regularly, but when she did lash out, first crockery would be smashed and then she would hit the girl in the face, without warning, on the mouth, in the eye. On her right hand she wore two large rings. This would be followed by scenes of atonement, the weeping mother and the weeping daughter, the recompense, the two or three glasses of wine that the daughter was allowed to drink in the evenings in front of the television, which was normally switched off out of principle.

She'd punched her twice: in the eye – which she hadn't fully connected with – and on the mouth.

The girl had fallen to her knees and then the woman had, as ever, felt sorry. When the girl stood up again she spat in her mother's face.

That had been on the evening before the girl disappeared with the boy who lived next door.

B oth the boy's parents came from the village. They'd always lived there, they didn't know anything different. The boy's father had been in a clinic for a week.

When the boy's mother heard from the bus driver, her ex-brother-in-law, that not only her son but also the girl from next door had failed to get on the bus that morning, she became less worried.

She was convinced that the boy had run away with the girl. He'd run away because of the girl. He wouldn't have a reason for running away on his own. The girl was the reason.

The boy's mother liked the girl. The boy's parents and the girl's mother knew each other but didn't have much contact.

When they were younger the boy and girl had often gone to the woods together, sometimes for the whole day. The boy's father used to have a hunting licence. When he still hunted, he'd sometimes taken the children with him.

The boy's father and mother used to wind cables in a factory twenty kilometres away. There was no more work for them in the area.

When the boy hadn't returned by evening the mother had called the police.

The policewoman, the girl's mother and the boy's mother stood in the dark by the village bus stop in the snow. They looked down the street.

"I reckon they went off to the woods," the boy's mother said. The girl's mother said nothing.

"The woods?" the policewoman said. "Why? If they're in the woods they'll be back in a few hours. They won't stay the night in the woods. Surely not." She laughed.

The boy's mother went back to her house and rang the clinic. It wasn't easy to reach the boy's father, especially in the evening. The patients didn't have their own telephones. They weren't allowed mobiles, they had to surrender them. On the long corridor on the ward there was a single telephone on the wall. You could call this number from outside, but either the number would be busy, often for hours on end, or nobody picked up.

"The boy's run away," she said. "With the girl. They've probably gone to the woods."

"The boy knows his way around the woods," the boy's father said.

"But in this snow . . ."

"The boy knows what he's doing. How long have they been missing?"

"Since about half six this morning. They didn't get on the bus."

"The boy knows what he's doing."

"Here everyone's talking about a wolf. Have you heard about the wolf?"

"Yes." He said yes, but he wasn't sure.

He couldn't remember.

"There's a wolf in the area."

"A wolf, yes . . ."

"Someone's got to go after them."

"They won't let me out of here. I can't get out."

He sounded tired and sober. Years ago, before the cable factory, he used to work in the woods.

Most men in the village drank, the women too, but he drank more than the others. He'd been on the way to killing himself with schnapps. Ten days ago he'd drunk so much that he'd walked onto the tracks at the station in Beeskow. He'd stood on the tracks, shouting at the top of his voice. The trains stopped outside Beeskow and four transport police officers came to remove him from the tracks. He was taken to the psychiatric clinic in Frankfurt an der Oder and put on a closed ward. He had to be tied down to the bed. Later he couldn't remember the railway tracks nor the first few days in the psychiatric clinic, tied to a bed. After three days he was sober but exhausted. He had stopped shaking. The call came a week later. He was standing by the patient telephone in the long corridor of the closed ward.

"They won't let me out of here."

"Someone's got to go looking for them, nobody's looking

for them. The police say they'll turn up."

"I won't get out of here."

He paused briefly.

"I wouldn't make it either."

The following day the boy's father was transferred to a different ward. The senior doctor was in his mid-thirties at most. He wore cowboy boots. The boy's father explained the situation to him. He said he had to go, even though he didn't want to.

"Next time you'll be under the train," the doctor said.

The following morning the boy and girl ate snow to combat their thirst. They set off again, but they felt the exertions of the previous day and they were hungry. Their progress was slow.

At the edge of a field they found a corpse at the bottom of a ladder leading up to a hide.

The dead hunter lay on his back in the snow, his eyes open.

From Vierlinden bei Seelow, where a hunter had first seen his tracks, the wolf moved in an arc southwards, and from there slowly to the north-west, towards Berlin. His tracks were found in Falkenhagen, in Berkenbrück, then the wolf must have crossed the motorway several times around February 16. In the night of February 16–17 Tomasz had photographed him. Later, more tracks were found at Spreehagen and then at Woltersdorf.

The wolf hunted hares and rabbits, deer, but the deep snow slowed him down and hunting became more difficult. Hunger drove him closer to humankind. At night he ate rubbish that he found in the rest areas by the side of the motorway.

"Did you hear that?"

"Hear what, Charly?"

Charly opened his eyes wide again in a bizarre way.

"You look really weird, Charly."

"Come on, let's go outside."

"It's snowing outside," Jacky said.

"Come on, let's go out and have a fag. Have you heard about the wolf? Haven't you seen the photo?"

"What's up with you, Charly? You're so nervous."

"Yeah, I don't know, I'm nervous, I feel something's coming, but I don't know what, and then there's this thing with the wolf, a wolf outside Berlin, here on the photo, eighty kilometres from Berlin, and now maybe it's only sixty or fifty or forty kilometres away, and at some point it'll be here, in Adlershof or Hönow or Marzahn or Lichtenberg or Ahrensfelde, just imagine that, it's coming from the east, I mean, what if? Think it through, just imagine."

Jacky went into the kiosk and sold a man a packet of cigarettes. Charly waited outside. She came back out.

*

"I always think of us as the eyes."

"The eyes, Charly?"

"The eyes of the city."

"What do you mean?"

"I mean that everything is here, all knowledge, every piece of news, every image, and we're a part of the neighbourhood, we know the names of the people here, we take in packages for them, we know what they get sent and we know what they buy from us, during the day and at night, and in the daytime they buy different things from at night, beer, vodka and cigarettes, and we know how much vodka they buy and how many lottery tickets they fill out."

They were standing in the entrance to their shop. Behind them the lottery advertisement glowed yellow.

"Don't you understand?"

Jacky didn't understand him. She had an inkling of what he meant, but she wasn't sure. She looked at him and laughed.

"What now?"

"I think we have to watch out, or we'll no longer be the eyes."

"But . . ."

"If we don't watch out, this is what I'm saying, and then . . . I wonder, Jacky, I wonder who's taking the photos. Can you answer that? Can you tell me who's taking the photos?"

He paused briefly.

"The people who come in here, they're newspaper people, they're telly people, or they're some sort of people, who knows what sort of people they are, but they're people who weren't here before, they take the photos and they print the photos, and then, well, then the photo is in your head. Did you see that photo in the paper of the wolf outside Berlin? There's only one picture of it, and it's everywhere. So who took it? Why didn't we take it, Jacky? *We* are the eyes."

They stood a moment longer in the entrance to the shop, staring out into the snow.

The longer Tomasz was in Berlin, the more difficult he found it to be alone. He got scared when he was alone. He was frightened, but he didn't know what of.

Agnieszka started work at six o'clock every morning, but because of the noise they didn't start on the building site till seven. That meant he was alone for an hour. So he got up with her and took her to work, every day, to a couple in Dahlem, where she cleaned and did the housework every morning from six till nine. He parked the car in front of the villa, she went into the house and he waited in the Toyota until it was time to drive on to the building site. She couldn't take him into the house with her.

The people Agnieszka cleaned for every morning were artists. He was a painter and sculptor, she a sculptress, he was in his late fifties or early sixties, she about forty. They had a lot of money.

"I'd like to paint you," the man, the artist, always said to Agnieszka. He said it almost every day.

"No, I don't want that," was always her answer.

"Why don't you model for him?" the man's wife, an oriental

woman, would say. "It's easy money."

Every day Tomasz waited outside the villa in the old Toyota until twenty to seven, before driving to the building site. By the time his colleagues arrived his first panic attack of the day had already passed.

"Here he is, the prodigal son," they'd said, Marek and his men, when Tomasz returned the day before.

At six o'clock the previous morning, the man and woman for whom Agnieszka cleaned every day had been sitting in their kitchen, not having gone to bed, and the man had said by way of a greeting, "Sit down with us."

"We've just come back from Paris," he'd said, the painter. "Let's celebrate. There's always something to celebrate."

The man and woman took photographs of each other, of the full ashtray, the almost empty bottle, the woman's smudged eye shadow.

"I'd really love to paint a picture of you, so let me at least take a photo."

"My boyfriend took a photo of a wolf," Agnieszka said. "A few hours ago."

"Really?" he said. "Where?"

"On the motorway."

When Agnieszka arrives at six o'clock the following morning there is nobody at home, but various photographs are hanging up in the kitchen, 13 x 9-centimetre prints. They are the pictures from yesterday morning. On one of them the man, long grey hair, glasses, beard, heavyset, cigarette in one hand, glass of wine in the other. On another photograph his wife, the oriental woman, at the kitchen table, dark hair tied-up, smudged eye shadow, wearing the long, narrow dress she'd worn the day before. In the third photo Agnieszka, standing at the fridge. In the picture she's wearing what she always wears to work, on this day too as she's looking at the photo, grey tracksuit bottoms, a loose T-shirt. Her hair is up, she's wiping the door of the silver fridge with a cloth. She's smiling.

The photograph of the wolf on the motorway at night was on the front page and the newspaper was lying around during their breakfast break, at nine o'clock. Tomasz said to Marek, the boss, "I took that photo, they've even printed my name."

And Marek said, "You see, you see, I always said you'd be something one day. You're going to be famous."

Tomasz knew that Agnieszka was finished at the villa in Dahlem at nine. He called her every morning at five past, when she was on her way to the U-Bahn, and at around a quarter past nine she would get a train to the east of the city.

"Yes, everything's fine," she said on the telephone. "How about you?"

"I'm fine too."

"See you later, then."

The man lay dead on his back in the snow. His eyes were open. Partially under him was a rucksack, beside him in the snow a rifle. In the rucksack the boy and girl found tea, some food, half a bottle of schnapps and some money. They drank the tea and the schnapps, and quickly ate everything they found. They left the rucksack beside the body, but took the gun with them.

"I wonder where the dog is?" she said later as they were walking through the forest.

"Which dog?"

"The hunter. The hunter didn't have a dog with him."

At around midday they came to a little cemetery in the forest. They were hungry and thirsty. The tap outside the small chapel was frozen. The chapel was locked, but the door gave way when the boy rammed his shoulder against it. Inside the chapel they found woollen blankets on the pews. To the side were two electric heaters that weren't plugged in. In a small side room there was running water.

They stayed in the cemetery for several hours. They

plugged in the heaters. They undressed and tried to dry their wet things. They sat next to the heaters under the woollen blankets and waited. The boy had leaned the rifle against the wall. It got dark. They'd left the door half open so they could see if someone was coming, but nobody did.

Outside, the few crosses marking graves in the snow.

The light from a lantern angled in through the door. It had begun to snow again.

When their clothes were dry they set off, taking two of the woollen blankets with them. In the dark they came to a road, which they followed until they saw the lights of a petrol station at the edge of a village in the distance. They reckoned they were close to Storkow. Storkow had a train station.

He had been away for four weeks. When Tomasz was in Poland he didn't call as often, generally twice a day, not every two hours. He didn't call so often because in Poland he had people who talked to him and looked after him. His mother. His brother. Agnieszka's brother and his wife.

In the four weeks that Tomasz had been in Poland, Agnieszka had worked around the clock as usual, and on the Saturday evenings had gone dancing with her friend Janina.

On the telephone he'd tried to dissuade her from going.

He'd said he was forbidding her, said he'd jump into the car and drag her out of there by the hair, and then she'd screamed down the phone at him, for the first time in her life.

They hadn't spoken about it again. And that was the end of it. That was the end of his calls, too – apart from on Saturdays and Sundays.

Tomasz spent Saturday evenings with Agnieszka's brother and his wife in their sitting room, saying almost nothing, until at some point they sent him home. He slept at his mother's house, went with her to Mass on Sunday morning, and sometimes again in the evening. On Saturdays he sat motionless on the sofa at Agnieszka's brother's, on Sundays he sat motionless in Mass.

Then, at five o'clock on Monday, Agnieszka's telephone rang in Berlin.

On the first Saturday without him – the day she'd screamed down the phone at him – she'd met, with her friend Janina, a group of guys from Hellersdorf: electricians and car mechanics. The four of them were funny, they had short hair and well-toned bodies. Sometimes they spoke too quickly – Agnieszka didn't understand everything they said – and they had their own language, they used words that Agnieszka didn't know, words such as "wheels", which meant "car", or "cheeba", which meant "weed".

She went back to the club with Janina the following weekend and the boys turned up again around midnight. They stayed at the club until three and then moved on. The guys had cars. Eventually all six of them ended up in a tower block in Hellersdorf where they watched the sun come up. They drank vodka and smoked cheeba.

One of the guys was called Andi. Andi and Agnieszka started kissing and after a while his hand found its way inside her trousers.

"Next time you'll be under the train," the senior doctor had said. "What's going to happen if nobody picks you up off the tracks next time?" The doctor was gazing out of the window. He was keeping the next patient waiting. He'd been keeping him waiting for ten minutes now. He returned to his desk, closed the file, opened it again and closed it. He placed the file on a small table beside the desk, which already carried a heap of other files. On the wall hung a picture a friend had painted of him. Sometimes he liked it, sometimes he didn't.

The doctor stood up again and looked out of the window. He'd told the man what would happen. That he wouldn't have a chance, not a sniff of a chance, as they said in English. Sometimes English terms came to mind, phrases, bits of sentences such as "in the wee small hours". He'd worked in Toronto for four years, in research, and now he was here. Without a family he would have stayed in Canada.

He thought of his wife and two children. He wondered why he wasn't going back to Canada with his family.

He thought of the story with the wolf.

At night foxes came close to the clinic. Nobody here had

seen the wolf, but they were all talking about him.

His wife, the children. The children had asked if the wolf could come to their house. No, he'd said. The house is made of stone.

Is it true that in America all the houses are made of wood? Yes, lots are. But not all of them.

He'd told the man what would happen and that it was just a matter of days before they'd be seeing each other again. That everything would be back to square one.

He tried to think how many people he'd helped as a doctor. Not a single one, the doctor thought, even though he knew this wasn't true. But he'd never *really* helped anyone. He'd just shifted time. He'd given up aspiring to achieve more than that. And maybe that was sufficient. Shifting time, always a little further forwards.

No, he then thought. Of course that wasn't enough. But he wasn't capable of achieving more, in the best-case scenario that was all he could do. He thought of houses made of straw and houses made of wood and houses made of stone. He thought how often he might have been wrong in his life. Maybe you couldn't help anybody. He wondered which doctor had helped him.

Dentists help. But dentists commit suicide. Psychiatrists help, and psychiatrists kill themselves too.

Yes, he thought, you can help if it's not too late. But from what point can you no longer help? Maybe from the very start it's already too late.

With drinkers there were no mistakes. With drinkers you could merely shift time, every one of them caved in again sooner or later.

Agnieszka got onto the U-Bahn at nine seventeen. She found a seat and tapped a message into her mobile. She typed the characters 9, full stop, 1 and 7. For the last few days she and the guy from the club had been sending each other messages like this, messages like 14.02 or 07.15 or 03.42. Nine point one seven meant: it's nine seventeen and at this very moment I'm thinking of you.

He replied a little later: 9.29, and then, before she arrived in Prenzlauer Berg, she wrote back: 9.46. She got off the train and took a short detour via a chemist's before going to the next apartment she was due to clean. Nobody was in.

At ten zero one she wrote: 10.01. And then she added: I might be pregnant.

On the afternoon of the day following the telephone call, the boy's father was back in the village. From the kitchen window his wife saw him coming down the street. He hadn't rung. He went inside, got changed, packed a few things, rucksack, supplies, a torch, a large-bladed hunting knife. His wife stood in the hall, watching him pack. He had thin grey hair. His face was broad and unshaven. He was in his mid-fifties, just like her. They barely exchanged a word.

She said he looked tired.

He was sober for the first time in years, and he was afraid of a relapse. On the kitchen table stood a bottle of vodka.

He couldn't stand being in this house. Things looked different. His wife looked different. The light was different.

He set off immediately. It was still light.

First he went to the bus stop and from there took the shortest route to the edge of the woods. It was what the children would have done too.

At the edge of the woods he found boot prints in the snow and followed them. He was soon out of breath. The man hadn't walked so far in years. He had to keep stopping. His thoughts kept returning to the young doctor's boots.

He found the butts of roll-ups. It got dark, but he kept going. The snow was bright enough, he didn't need the torch. He found the trailer. He was utterly exhausted, his knees were trembling, but after another break he continued into the night. He kept following the boot prints and saw other tracks too, tracks of deer, hares, dogs, they may even have been wolf tracks, but then it started snowing again and the tracks became more and more difficult to identify. He was scared of a relapse, which is why he didn't turn back.

He couldn't help thinking once more of the doctor's boots and in his head he heard the voice of the man, in a dialect he did not like. He walked through the snow, able to recall things, faces, names, images he hadn't thought about for decades.

The children's tracks took him on and on. He knew he wouldn't catch up with them. He assumed they'd slept in the trailer and then continued walking in the morning. There wasn't a secret treehouse, no hut or cave where they could be hiding – they were plodding onwards and they had more than a day's head start. The man stopped. He decided to turn around and sleep in the trailer.

Then he saw the man lying in the snow beside a ladder to a hide.

"You're going to be famous," Marek had said.

Marek and his team were gutting and renovating an entire apartment building in Lychener Strasse. Lychener Strasse is in the north of Berlin's Prenzlauer Berg. In the past, before the Second World War, Prenzlauer Berg used to be a workers' quarter. On every floor of the house there had been three small apartments, each with a coal oven. Now Marek and his team were tearing down the walls and making three apartments into two, or making three apartments into one, or at the top of the building turning two floors into one apartment. It was only on the ground floor that they weren't doing anything, as still living there were an old couple who refused to move out because they'd been living in that apartment for almost seventy years. They were there before the war, and they'd lived there during the time of the German Democratic Republic. Both of them were over ninety. They'd been offered a replacement apartment, which they'd rejected.

Eventually their electricity and water were cut off, but still the old couple wouldn't leave.

The rest of the house looked more like a ruin every day.

Marek and his men were ripping out everything, the partition walls, the windows. Tomasz and the others stood amongst the debris and dust, working with sledgehammers and cutters. They wore white protective masks, but these didn't help much. They had dust in their eyes, in their hair, in their mouths, everywhere.

After tearing down the walls they tore off layers of pasteboard, lino and mouldy carpet from the old, broken floorboards. In some of the apartments they found things, they found old newspapers, books, entire cupboards. In one apartment they found a kitchen drawer full of letters, and in another a record player and a dead bird in a cage.

"Look at that, boss," Tomasz said, and Marek said:

"Better a dead bird in a cage than a skeleton in the attic."

Tomasz didn't laugh because he didn't know the saying.

"Or in the cupboard," Marek added afterwards.

In the attic of the house they found an old cash register.

In the cellar they found coal, empty bottles, mattresses, broken chairs, a scythe and a mortar.

In an apartment on the fourth floor someone had scribbled on all the walls, doors, window frames, while in an apartment on the second floor someone had scratched a large swastika.

The Polish workers ripped out everything, the sinks, the tiles, the lino floors, the windows.

"Don't forget to check inside the coal stoves to see if there's anything there," Marek said, and in fact Tomasz did find a shallow box in one of them. Inside the box were old toys and keys and photographs and a pocket watch.

They gutted the building floor by floor, only load-bearing walls remained, each storey became a large, high room with empty window openings through which the dust flew.

Marek didn't really get on with men like Tomasz – he didn't have much of a sense of humour – but he rated him as a foreman. Tomasz worked faster and harder than the others, he didn't talk and he didn't drink. He said virtually nothing at all.

Tomasz didn't have anything to say, but he talked a lot in his head as he tore the walls down. He talked to his mother, he talked to his brother and he talked to Agnieszka's brother, or he talked to Agnieszka herself. He talked about wanting to live a different life, wondering how things would turn out, what the future had in store, whether he and Agnieszka ought to get married, whether they might have children and where these children should live, in Berlin, Warsaw, Poland, or somewhere else.

The man was dead. He was lying on his back, facing upwards, eyes open. The man's rucksack was beside him in the snow. No dog, no traces of a dog. No gun. The boy's father thought he recognised the dead man. He was sure he knew him, but he couldn't say from where. Not from the village. Maybe from Pfaffendorf or Neubrück. It was still snowing. The man knew that he wouldn't be able to continue following the children's tracks.

In his head he had the voice of the senior doctor, the voice of the night nurse, the voice of a Russian he'd known thirty-five years ago. He didn't want to leave the corpse alone under the blanket of snow. The boy's father climbed up into the hide. The sleeping bag was warm enough. He sat in the hide and gazed out at the white field of snow in the night. Occasionally he glanced down at the dead man, but by now he could barely make out the body beneath the covering of snow. He wondered what was in the dead man's rucksack. He was certain he would find schnapps in the rucksack – a bottle or a hipflask. Everyone who went into the woods in winter took schnapps with them.

*

The senior doctor's boots. The dialect he didn't like. He remembered a woman from Reichenwalde with whom he'd gone to a lake in the woods when he was younger. He thought of the wolf, of the wolf's tracks in the snow. He'd never seen a wolf. He knew that there were wolves further south, in Lusatia, but not here. He spoke quietly to himself and he spoke quietly to the dead man in the snow. We have to report this, we have to tell them. So that no-one misses you. So that no-one goes looking for you. Where's your dog?

He thought again of the doctor and then remembered an occasion – he may have been nineteen or twenty – when he'd looked in the mirror. This was during his time in the army, in a barracks, he'd already started drinking by then. He had looked in the mirror, he remembered how in the barracks as a young man with close-cropped hair, drunk, but lucid enough, he had looked himself in the eye and how he'd kept doing that over the years – gazing drunkenly at himself for as long as his gaze remained lucid enough.

He couldn't remember the train station. He couldn't remember standing on the tracks. They'd told him about it in hospital, but he remembered nothing of the episode. He had no memory.

He could barely remember the past ten years. He'd had practically nothing to do with the boy. When the boy was younger, they'd sometimes gone into the woods together. With the girl, too.

Maybe he knew the dead man from his time in the army. He was certain that there must be schnapps somewhere in the rucksack. There hadn't been a gun. The children had taken the gun.

The doctor's dialect. We have to report it, we have to tell them. Next time you'll be under the train. We have to tell someone. He didn't have a phone. His phone had been missing for weeks. He couldn't remember how he'd got to the station in Beeskow, or who he'd been with. Maybe there was a mobile in the dead man's rucksack. Maybe there was a bottle of schnapps in the dead man's rucksack.

The man fell asleep and dreamed of a spider and a stag beetle, but in his dream the stag beetle had a green shimmer.

The messages on Agnieszka's mobile:

14.31

14.47

15.55

17.02

17.03

20.11

20.20

20.22

At seven o'clock in the evening they stopped work at the building site. Marek unplugged the spotlights and then the eight men went down the four floors. Tomasz turned back halfway, he'd forgotten his hat. He had been brought up not to leave his belongings lying around just anywhere. He hurried back up to the fourth floor and looked for his hat, but couldn't find it in the darkness. He abandoned his search and went back down the four floors in the dark stairwell. The others had gone. On the ground floor the door of the still-inhabited apartment was ajar. Tomasz stopped in the dark stairwell. He saw a half-naked old man cutting up a *Fleischwurst* at a small table by the light of a candle, and then tossing the pieces onto the floor. Tomasz knew that a woman lived in the apartment too, but he couldn't see or hear her. Tomasz stood for a while in the stairwell, watching the man. Then he saw the old lady, bent double and almost toothless. In one hand she held a poker and in the other a bucket.

Tomasz went on his way, leaving the building and getting into his car. He drove to Agnieszka, who every evening cleaned two open-plan offices on Rosa-Luxemburg-Platz.

He said more when he was with Agnieszka, at least more than on the building site, but still he didn't say much. He didn't say much about what he'd told her and his mother and her brother. In his head.

Often he just looked at her. He would stand holding the vacuum cleaner in the open-plan office between the empty work stations and just look at her. At some point she'd say: Come on, keep going.

They hurried to the petrol station in the dark. Cars flashed their headlights, hooted, overtook them. In their black clothes the girl and boy were barely visible at the side of the road. He was carrying the rifle across his shoulder, wrapped in one of the blankets from the chapel. The rifle was heavy.

They reached the place-name sign at the edge of the town, after which there was a narrow curb and streetlights.

Although they knew the petrol station was expensive, they were thirsty and hungry and couldn't go without food any longer. He waited outside in the light of the fluorescent lamps, while she went in. She bought water, crisps, chocolate and tobacco.

They stood briefly beneath a streetlight on the other side of the petrol station and ripped open the packaging. It was snowing. They didn't know where to go – into town and to the station, or back into the woods. They felt sure that they'd be apprehended at the station.

She said they wouldn't survive another night in the woods.

A car stopped. A man with long, thin hair and a beard reached across the passenger seat and opened the car window. The man was in his mid-forties and his face looked white in the light of the streetlamp. They didn't know him.

"I'll give you a lift, if you like," the man said.

She sat in the passenger seat, the boy got into the back. It was an old car. A Renault, the doors got stuck. The boy put the rifle wrapped in a blanket by his feet.

"Where do you want to go?" the man with the long hair asked.

"I don't know," she said.

For a while nobody spoke. The car stereo was off.

"If you like you could spend the night at my place. I live on a farm, about twenty kilometres from here. You can have a shower and I'll make you something to eat. You could get warm. It's too cold outside. Too much snow. Tomorrow morning I'll take you to the station. I have to go in that direction anyway."

The boy didn't say anything.

"O.K.," the girl said after a while.

A pause.

"Where do you come from?" the man asked.

"Sauen."

"Sauen. Did you come by bus?"

"We walked," she said.

"Walked?" After that the man said nothing for a time. "You can have a shower at mine. I'll make you something to eat. I've got enough room."

"Thanks," the girl said.

"I used to be a teacher," the man said after a while. "In Berlin. Are you both still at school?"

Neither gave an answer.

"I'm not a teacher anymore. I couldn't take it any longer."

He laughed. The two children laughed as well.

The lights of the town were now well behind them and they were back on the highway. They drove across a bridge.

"Was that the motorway?" the boy asked.

"That was the motorway," the man said.

They drove for another ten minutes until they arrived at his place. He lived in a small, poorly rendered house at the edge of a village. Nobody had looked after the place for years. The window frames were rotten, as were the doors. The man had barely any furniture. The few items he did have he'd collected from somewhere. In the sitting room there was a broken table with a hole in the top and a few chairs.

"How did the table get that hole in it?!" the girl said.

"No idea. It looks as if someone set about it with a hammer."

An old sofa, an armchair. No cupboards, no shelves. Everything the man owned lay on the floor or was stowed in removal boxes. On one wall hung the famous picture of Che Guevara, on another a photograph of a Russian icon.

"You've got a black eye," the man said.

The man lived alone. The boy and girl showered while the man prepared the food.

They showered together. The boy didn't trust the man. He took the rifle wrapped in the woollen blanket into the bathroom and locked the door.

The man heated up some tins of ravioli, he didn't have anything else. After they'd eaten they sat on the sofa and in the armchair and smoked.

"I've seen the wolf, you know. Well, I think I saw the wolf. Have you heard about the wolf? There's a wolf somewhere around here. I think I saw it."

"What couldn't you take anymore?" the girl said.

"What?" he said. "What did you say?"

"What couldn't you take anymore? As a teacher."

"I think I really did see it," the man said.

He looked gaunt. Bad skin. He opened a bottle of wine, which the three of them drank quickly, then he opened a second one. He sat in the broken armchair.

"I couldn't take the children anymore. The children and the parents. I don't think I was a particularly good teacher."

They slept in an adjacent room on old, damp mattresses on the floor.

"Do you often have guests?" she said to him.

"Sometimes," he said. "Not that often."

He paused.

"I do what I can. Tomorrow I'll drive you to the station."

Two days after Tomasz had taken the photograph at the side of the motorway the wolf was spotted near Woltersdorf. He was moving slowly northwards now. He'd crossed the orbital motorway and was almost in the Berlin metropolitan area.

The newspapers were full of the story, the wolf had names or nicknames. The city was abuzz with excitement. The stray wolf in winter. The stray wolf on his way to Berlin.

They spoke of sedating and capturing the wolf, and taking it back to where it had come from, but nobody in the area had any experience with wolves and you couldn't rule out the possibility that the animal might have rabies, because wolves usually avoid cities – unless, perhaps, they've got rabies. A wolf in the city or near the city was dangerous.

"If you've got to do it, you've got to do it," Jacky had said the day after the photograph appeared in the papers, "We are the eyes, Jacky," and then at six o'clock the following morning Charly, rather than bringing in the papers and opening up the shop, had driven to the edge of the city, to the north-east, where the Marzahn high-rise estates stop and the fields and wasteland begin on the other side of the road.

He had grown up here, and here, in front of or between the tower blocks and the small, old and derelict semi-detached houses, the wolf was going to appear, Charly saw the image in his mind, he knew it.

"I just know it, Jacky, I can see it, I can see it in my head."

Traces of the wolf had been seen outside Woltersdorf, and before that near Spreenhagen, which meant he was heading north-westwards, getting ever closer to the city, although he wasn't going in a straight line as he was seeking out woods and forestry plantations. Essentially he was seeking prey and scavenging in rubbish.

Charly knew where the wolf had left his tracks most

recently, he even had a map on which he'd marked the wolf's route so far. He was convinced that the creature would turn up here in the north-east, near Marzahn. He drove to Blumberger Damm and stopped in Golliner Strasse. It was still dark, it was cold and it had started snowing again. But he got out of the car and waited.

Charly knew nothing about wolves. He'd never seen one close up.

He stood beside the car and gazed out at the fields between Marzahn, Hönow and Ahrensfelde, but in the driving snow he couldn't make out very much.

It was early, between six and seven.

Occasionally he turned and saw individual lights go on or off in the tower blocks behind him. Then he looked back towards the east and south-east, peering into the darkness at the fields.

Charly's plan changed from one moment to the next. He had the sudden feeling that he'd made a mistake. He leaped back into the car. He kept driving along the perimeter of the city and then headed for Mehrow. His mobile rang, it was the melody of a harp, the ringtone when Jacky called. Charly was on the road between Ahrensfelde and Hoheneiche. He pulled over on the right and switched off the engine.

"Where are you?"

"You know where I am."

"But when did you leave?"

"I told you I was going to take a drive out of town."

"Yes, you did, Charly, but you didn't say when. I woke up and thought, where the hell is he, why's he not having a lie-in because Peter's opening up today? It's Thursday, after all—"

"But it's not Thursday today."

"Huh?"

"What do you mean, Huh?"

"What day is it then?"

"What makes you think it's Thursday? Today's Wednesday."

"Wednesday?"

"You've got your days mixed up. It's not Thursday today."

"But if it's Wednesday and not Thursday, why didn't you open up the shop?"

"Because we agreed that you'd do it."

While Charly was talking to Jacky he looked at the fields and a small path that turned off from the road and led across the fields towards the east.

Dawn broke. Further south he could see the neon sign of a petrol station, but in fact he was staring into nothing.

"That's what we agreed." And then bizarrely he wrenched his eyes wide open again, a tic, a nervous thing, but it felt nice in the corners of his eyes, it hurt a little and woke him up.

"Jacky, I've got to keep going." He put his mobile away and was about to turn on the ignition, but instead got out of the car. It was just before seven o'clock. It would soon be light.

The wolf came from the south-east. He came across one of the fields and then loped along the road towards the tower blocks in the distance. He didn't slow down, nor did he speed up. He was walking along the other side of the road and heading towards Charly, but Charly didn't see him until he was no more than ten metres away. Charly froze. The wolf was larger than he'd imagined.

Although Charly had the camera around his neck, he was paralysed by fear. He couldn't move. He couldn't take the picture. It was only when he was five or six metres away that the wolf stopped. The wolf was big and scraggy. He stood there motionless, staring at Charly.

Charly was desperate to lift up the camera and take a photo, but he couldn't. He couldn't move.

All of a sudden the wolf moved very quickly.

He crossed the carriageway, leaped over the roadside ditch and sprinted across a field towards the west, in the direction of Eiche and Marzahn. Charly had to run around the car in order to photograph the beast, but he was already too far away. A dark dot in the snow. Charly yelled after the wolf.

Tomasz had driven her to the villa in Dahlem. It was early in the morning, just before six – the third morning since his return to Berlin. He stopped outside the house, but she didn't get out straightaway as usual. He switched off the engine. She looked at him.

"I'm pregnant," she said. "But it's not your baby. It's another man's."

She didn't say any more. Grabbing her bag, she got out of the car and went up to the entrance. She unlocked the front door to the villa and disappeared inside the house. Tomasz started the engine and drove back to their apartment. He packed up the few things in the apartment that belonged to him, placed the key on the kitchen table and shut the door behind him.

He drove to the building site. Marek looked at him and asked whether everything was alright. Tomasz nodded.

The next morning it had snowed so much that it was impossible to go on following the children's footprints.

The dead man lay under a twenty-centimetre shroud of snow.

There was no point. The boy's father knew he had to find a telephone, but he didn't want to return to the village. Back at the house, with his wife, he would immediately start drinking again. He kept going. He wasn't looking for footprints anymore, but for a forest path. After two hours he came to a village and rang the bell at one of the farms. A broad-shouldered man opened the door, a man around his age or somewhat older. It was just before ten in the morning. The man let him in.

It took a while before the police and ambulance arrived. They wanted to go in the patrol car along the forest road, but the snow on the ground made it impossible. The wheels spun. They had to walk. The boy's father led the police to the hide. The policemen took his name. One of them said he knew the boy's father, but the boy's father couldn't remember the policeman. They asked whether he knew the dead man, they kept asking him this. They couldn't believe that he didn't know the dead man. Over and over again he told them how he'd found the body. Finally he was allowed to go. He left the policemen and paramedics in the snow at the edge of the clearing and wandered along the forest road until he came back to the village from where he'd called the police. It was now afternoon. The boy's father was hungry.

He rang again at the same house, and again the broad-shouldered man opened the door with a bottle of beer in his hand. The boy's father asked whether he could use the telephone again. While he stood by the telephone in the hallway, waiting for his wife to pick up, the man holding the bottle of beer sat in the kitchen listening to the radio.

His wife didn't have any news, the children hadn't been apprehended and nobody had seen them.

"Where are you going to go now? What are you going to do? Or are you coming back home?" she said.

He could hear that she'd already had a drink or two.

"I don't know yet." He hung up, called out something from the hallway towards the kitchen, where he saw the man sitting at the table, and opened the front door. The broad-shouldered man came after him.

"Where are you going?" he asked.

"To the station."

"To Beeskow station?" The boy's father was already out on the road. The man was standing in the doorway with his beer. "I'll give you a lift," he said.

"I can walk," the boy's father said.

"Too far," the other man said. "Too far. I'll drive you." He put on an old coat.

He's glad to get out of the house, the boy's father thought. And then he thought that this had only occurred to him because he hadn't had a drink for nine days. The man had an old Lada. They drove in silence to Beeskow.

"So," the man said eventually. "Who was it then?"

"I don't know."

"What about the police?"

"They didn't recognise him either. A hunter."

"No way," the man driving said. "Did he top himself?"

"No."

She'd said she knew about wolves. This wasn't true, but she'd said it anyway. In the meeting the editor-in-chief had asked whether anyone knew about wolves and she was the only one to put her hand up, the intern. He had looked at her and she'd lied. She said she'd seen wolves as a child, in eastern Turkey. That was all made up because she'd never seen a wolf, nor had she ever lived in eastern Turkey. She was born in Berlin and had lived her entire life here. But she had heard about wolves. Her grandfather had gone wolf hunting, her father too, she thought, as a young man before her parents had moved here, but she herself had never seen a wolf in her life.

She was in her mid-twenties and trying to get a foot in the door at the newspaper. Her name was Semra.

She would write about the wolf even if she didn't have a clue about wolves, it didn't matter. This was her chance.

When the girl and boy awoke the next day the man was already in the kitchen. He'd made coffee. It was late, they'd slept more than half the day.

"Then I'll drive you to the train station. It snowed all night."

He was standing at the window. Holding the rifle. He must have taken it from the room next door during the night. He was just holding it, the barrel was pointing to the floor. He wasn't aiming it at them.

"I'll drive you to the station. But you can't take this thing with you." He paused. "You won't get very far with it."

"It's *ours*," the boy said. "Give it back."

"You can't take it with you. You can do what you want, I won't tell a soul that I've seen you. You can go where you please, I'll even give you money, but you can't take this with you."

"Why not?" the boy said.

"Give us the rifle back," the girl said.

"No way," the man said.

"Give us the rifle," the girl said.

"I'll give you money," the man with the beard said. "I'll buy it from you." The girl went for the man. She shoved him, and to begin with he defended himself with his free left hand, but then he gripped the gun with both hands and pushed the girl away with the butt. The boy intervened. The boy and the man fought for the rifle. Both were slim, thin. Both held on fast to the gun, trying to wrestle it from the other's hands. "Stop it," the man with the beard kept saying, "Let go," and then all of a sudden the boy did let go of the rifle and punched the man in the face twice, in quick succession. The back of the man's head hit the wall and he slumped to the floor in a daze. He was bleeding. His nose was bleeding and his lip was cut. He let go of the rifle and put his hands up to his face. His hands were covered in blood.

He was whimpering, almost crying. He remained sitting on the floor.

The boy took the gun. They fetched their things from the room next door, shoes, coats, the blankets from the chapel. The man with the long hair and beard was still sitting on the floor, saying nothing. The boy and girl ran out of the house. Right behind it was the edge of the forest.

They ran right through the forest. They were afraid that he would catch them up with his car if they stuck to the paths. They ran for an hour. Nobody was behind them. They didn't know where they were. They tried to get their bearings, but it was impossible. After another hour they came to an embankment and a fence. On the other side of the fence was a train.

The train was standing in the forest. A freight train waiting for a signal. The signal didn't come because further down the tracks was a stationary diesel locomotive.

The boy and girl stood by the fence, looking at the train. They found a place where they could crawl under the fence. Crouching, they walked alongside the goods train. Most of the cars were loaded with containers. On each wagon was a small platform behind the container, where the railway workers stood when they coupled the cars. The children climbed onto the platform of the last wagon and waited.

It was hours before the train slowly began to move again. When it gathered speed the two of them laughed, they shrieked with pleasure, they felt free.

But the train got ever faster and although they were sitting in the lee of the container, it was too cold on the platform. They still had the blankets from the chapel, but the airstream was too cold. Even though they pulled the blankets over their heads and huddled close together, the wind was still unbearable. The train was moving too quickly, now they couldn't leap off. They were scared to death. Both of them realised that they might not survive the journey on this icy platform.

The goods train had come from Frankfurt an der Oder and was on its way to Berlin.

The car belonging to the man in the village had stopped outside the train station in Beeskow. Dirty snow lay on the forecourt.

"It's supposed to be getting warmer in the next few days," the man said.

"Thanks for the lift," the boy's father said.

The man in the Lada went on his way.

The boy's father stood on the station forecourt. Ten days ago this was where he'd been found yelling on the railway tracks, after which he'd been taken to the psychiatric unit in Frankfurt an der Oder, but he couldn't remember any of it.

Right in front of him was the pub where, without being able to remember, he'd got utterly paralytic before clambering onto the tracks.

Men were standing outside the pub, smoking. He turned and walked away from the station. He walked through the town. It was market day in the central square, but there were only three or four stalls. On sale were household goods, cheap clothes and smoked fish. The boy's father bought himself something to eat.

*

He walked through the town, but it was a small place. When he found himself outside the station for the second time, he rang his wife again from a telephone booth on the station concourse. On the concourse was another entrance to the pub. Babsi's Station Snug.

His wife had no news. Since their conversation that morning she'd been gradually working her way through the vodka. She wasn't drunk, but he could hear it.

"I'll call again in an hour," he said.

The last thing he wanted was to go home, but where should he go? He'd lost the trail, he had no goal. He was cold. He sat on a bench on the station concourse. He felt as if people were staring at him, but maybe he was just imagining it. He could hear the drunken chatter of the men and women in the pub, but he couldn't understand what they were saying. He wanted a beer. Outside it gradually got dark. The station bus back to the village was leaving in twenty minutes. He wasn't sure if he'd take the bus and he wasn't sure what would happen if he didn't take the bus. Laughter and voices from the pub. The reek of cigarettes. The man wanted a beer, but he stayed on the bench on the concourse. He looked through the glass door onto the forecourt. He watched the arrival of the bus that was going back to his village, watched it stop and then move away again. There were only three people on the bus.

The boy's father stood up, took his rucksack and sleeping

bag and went over to the yellow departure timetable beside the entrance to the pub. There were still a few more trains today, the next one for Frankfurt an der Oder would leave in a few minutes. The boy's father put the rucksack and sleeping bag down beneath the yellow timetable and went onto the plaform. This was where they'd pulled him off the tracks ten days ago.

A voice over the loudspeaker announced the arrival of the train. He was alone on the platform, nobody else there, no guard, no railway workers, no police officers either. The lights of the train came ever closer. He could almost make out the contours of the engine.

The man turned and went back onto the concourse. His rucksack was still on the stone floor beneath the yellow time-table. There were still a few more trains today. It was only a few steps from the timetable to the entrance to the pub. The man went into the station pub.

The woman was in her late forties, but she looked younger, or at least she dressed younger, almost like a girl. Her face was that of a woman in her late forties. She was standing in a very large period apartment in Wilmersdorf. Two days earlier the woman's mother had dropped dead, suddenly, in her late seventies while shopping in a delicatessen on Ludwigkirchstrasse.

It had taken a while to find the daughter. Mother and daughter had not spoken for years. The daughter wasn't registered anywhere, it almost seemed as though she didn't exist, there was no address, no social security number, no health insurance, no telephone number. They discovered an address book in the dead woman's apartment and eventually found the telephone number of her ex-husband, but the couple had got divorced twenty-five years ago. The man lived outside Mexico City and he refused to deal with the matter, but he gave the authorities a telephone number for their daughter. This was the number of a woman in New York with whom the woman now standing alone in her mother's Wilmersdorf apartment had lived and for whom she'd worked as a babysitter some years ago. The woman in New York had an address for the woman who'd moved back to Germany years earlier, Lychener Strasse 81, Berlin – Prenzlauer Berg, right beside the city ring railway.

The woman's name was Nadine, but that's not what she called herself. She hated her name. She stood in the apartment in Ludwigkirchstrasse in Wilmersdorf – a huge apartment with old parquet floors and white-and-blue tiles in the kitchen that were more than a hundred years old, with a pantry and mouldings, with an ancient lift and a wide, wood-panelled staircase, a separate servants' entrance and two balconies.

Nadine's mother had outlived her second husband, a very wealthy art collector. The walls were hung with paintings by Cy Twombly and Gerhard Richter, but Nadine didn't know a great deal about art, even though she'd wanted to study it years ago. She never even completed her schooling.

Nadine's mother had collected art herself. She had collected ethnic art, especially from India, ever since Nadine could remember.

Nadine wasn't interested. She hated her mother and hated her inclinations. Her mother and father had left Nadine behind in Bavaria when she was thirteen. They'd gone to India to meditate.

They'd left the child some oats, pasta, quite a lot of money and a list of telephone numbers of relatives. Her father came back after a year, having separated from Nadine's mother. Her mother didn't return until three years later. She persuaded her daughter to leave school and go back with her to India to learn meditation. Nadine stayed there several months but fell ill, contracted hepatitis and in the end wanted to go back to Germany. For a while she lived with her father on a farm by Ammersee, and then the father went to Mexico and she was on her own again. Mother and daughter lost contact with each other. In India her mother met a young, very wealthy art collector. They travelled on together, to the Himalayas, through China, through Arabia and later to Morocco.

On a shelf in her dead mother's apartment Nadine found a long row of mostly black diaries.

She threw the diaries into a cardboard box and began to read them on the train journey home. She got out at Schönhauser Allee and carried the box on her shoulder to her apartment in Lychener Strasse. She'd already decided to destroy the diaries. She was just trying to decide how.

The last section of Lychener Strasse is a dead end. It leads from Stargarder Strasse to a fence, about two metres high, beyond which lies the ring railway. From the apartments at the end of the street you can see the railway trench and the trains that pass by day and night.

After it got dark the train arrived at Rummelsburg freight station to the south-east of Berlin. The train was moving almost at walking pace, but it didn't come to a standstill. The boy and girl wanted to jump off but could barely move for the cold. The station lights in the snow drifted past them. They passed close by a group of railway workers who, illuminated by floodlights, were hauling cables beneath a bridge, then the train gathered speed a little, before stopping on a siding in the old freight station of Greifswalder Strasse.

Two policemen were waiting there.

One of the workers beneath the bridge in Rummelsburg had spotted the pair of crouching children on the train.

The girl and boy didn't know where they'd ended up. They climbed down from the train as best they could and walked woozily across the tracks towards the light of a lamp. Then they spotted the two transport police officers who'd been waiting for them. Both men were over fifty and both were overweight. The girl and boy would have been quicker than the policemen, but neither of them had any strength left. They were hungry, thirsty, almost numb from the wind and they were completely frozen. The two police officers took them to a shed beside the tracks. It was warm inside the shed. They were given water and blankets, but nobody called a doctor.

The boy answered the policemen's questions – What are your names, where have you come from, how did you get on the train? – while the girl slept under the blankets on a bench in the shed's neon lighting. The boy had forgotten the rifle when they'd climbed down from the train. He looked through the window. By now he'd realised that they were in Berlin. Inside the shed it smelled of burnt rubber.

He'd told the policemen everything they wanted to know.

"What happens now?" he said.

"What happens now?" one of the policemen said. "Wait and see."

The girl was sleeping.

One of the policemen left the room and the other had his back to the boy and girl because he couldn't get the kettle to work. The cable had melted. When he turned around the girl had woken up.

"Where do you think you're going? Stay here," the policeman called out.

The girl and boy ran through the station in the snow. The policeman stood at the door of the shed and called after them until they'd vanished into the darkness. When the second policeman returned the two officers drove in their car around the freight station and the surrounding area, but they did not find the two children.

The boy ran between the long, stationary freight trains back to where he and the girl had climbed down from the platform. He found the rifle.

Nobody in the pub seemed to recognise him, not even the landlady. The landlady, Babsi, was standing at the other end of the bar, talking to someone, and didn't look over at first. When finally she turned to the man he ordered a beer.

"Bottle or draught?"

"Draught." From his stool he could watch the woman start to draw the beer.

"New keg," the woman behind the bar said.

The boy's father knew that if he started drinking now he wouldn't stop. He watched the woman slowly draw the beer, he looked around the pub, he saw the faces of the other drinkers, the flashing slot machine in the corner beside the palm plant, he heard everything, the noise of the machines, the radio playing, the talking, the laughter, and he felt excited and untroubled. He'd said he would call again in an hour, and that hour was now up. He decided to call her before the beer, because he wouldn't think of it afterwards.

"Be back in a sec," he said to the woman behind the counter. "Is there a phone here?" And the woman nodded towards the concourse, to the telephone from which the boy's father had rung his wife an hour earlier.

The man went to the telephone on the concourse and as he dialled he caught sight of his rucksack and sleeping bag, which were still on the floor under the yellow timetable.

By now his wife was drunk, but she answered straightaway.

"They've been spotted," she said.

"Where?" the man said.

"But they got away again."

He didn't say anything. She wasn't slurring, but she spoke differently. He could hear how happy she was, how relieved.

"In Berlin," she said. "They were found at an old freight station in Berlin, but they got away again. Ran away from the police. Greifswalder Strasse. I didn't know there was a freight station in Greifswalder Strasse, I can't work out where it would be. Where are you going now? What are you doing now?"

"I don't know," the boy's father said.

The man hung up and went back to the yellow timetable. The next train to Berlin was leaving in ten minutes.

The boy's father looked through the glass door of the pub and saw the woman, Babsi, place his beer on the bar.

The telephone rang and someone told the girl's mother that the girl and boy had been spotted in Berlin. It was early evening. They wondered whether they ought to go round to the boy's parents' or whether they should ring them. In sixteen years they'd never had much to do with those people. The girl's mother didn't go round, but she rang them. The boy's mother was drunk. The police had already called her.

The girl's mother sat alone at her large, old kitchen table, smoking, looking out of the window and seeing in the glass a reflection of herself in the large kitchen with the old posters on the wall.

Two hours later, at half past ten, she got up, packed a few things, put on a coat and got into her car.

The border between East and West Berlin used to run between the northern end of Prenzlauer Berg and Wedding. Where the wall and the death strip once were is now the site of Mauerpark. To the north-west of Mauerpark, train tracks from all four points of the compass converge in a hollow.

At dusk on February 19, in this no-man's-land beneath Bösebrücke, around twenty commuters on various trains caught sight of the wolf, quite independently of each other.

Excited accounts later at dinner, I saw a wolf, have you heard about the wolf, what nonsense, just the other side of Gesundbrunnen, I saw him, I really did see him. Some people took photos, but most of them were too dark or too blurred. The wolf was too far away.

Still, on the basis of these multiple accounts, armed police with dogs combed the area, thereby unwittingly driving the wolf eastwards, without catching sight of him themselves, into the trench of the ring railway and towards Schönhauser Allee.

Tomasz worked that morning as if it were any other. He didn't say much, but he talked a great deal inside his head. He talked to his mother and Agnieszka's mother and Agnieszka's brother and Agnieszka.

It was a Wednesday. They'd ripped everything out of the house that it was possible to rip out.

"That's that done," Marek said. "We'll start again on Monday. Enjoy your long weekend."

The men left the building site, they went down the four floors, got into the minibus and drove with Marek across the border to Poland and back to their families. Tomasz left the building with the others, waited until they had gone, fetched his sleeping bag and mat from the boot of the Toyota and went back inside the house. He turned on the floodlight on the gutted fourth floor and switched on the small portable radio which played all day long on the building site.

He tried to remain calm, but couldn't manage it.

He realised he wouldn't be able to make it through the next few days alone. He wouldn't cope with being alone. He felt scared.

He thought about driving back to Agnieszka's apartment or to the open-plan office where she would start work in a couple of hours.

He went back down the stairs in the darkness. Once again the old couple's front door on the ground floor was open. Once again Tomasz stopped on the stairs and peered into their hallway. He couldn't see anyone, but he heard a radio and something like a whimpering or squealing. The sound reminded him of an unoiled bike, but it may have been the sound of an animal.

"Charly, you're doing that thing with your eyes again."

"The look, do you understand? The look . . ."

During the course of the day he'd told the story time and again, over and over, he couldn't stop. He told their regular customers and sometimes even strangers. He'd called a newspaper and told them that he'd seen the wolf near Marzahn, in the thick snow, not five metres away. The newspaper had sent an intern, a trainee as she introduced herself, a trainee, a young Turkish woman, he told her the story as well, and then she asked why he hadn't taken a photo.

He described the encounter with the wolf once more, explaining how he hadn't been able to take a photo even though he'd been holding the camera.

In the afternoon the shop was empty for a moment. Charly looked at Jacky.

"The look won't leave me alone. The look, Jacky, the eyes – I've never seen anything like it. The look was so cold. I hadn't expected that."

For a moment he stared into space. She didn't say anything and then he did the thing with his eyes again.

"She didn't believe me. But it was there, Jacky, I saw it, it was right there, I knew it, I have a feeling for things like that, I just didn't see it coming, it was there so suddenly, I felt paralysed, Jacky, it could have killed me, I tell you, I wasn't able to take a photo, but I did see it."

She said: "Yes, Charly, you knew. You knew and I knew that you knew."

The afternoon wore on, they sold newspapers and cigarettes, beer and sweets and schnapps.

"What did you feel?" the intern had said. He'd been afraid. In a way he'd been afraid like he'd never been afraid before.

The creature had stood before him. From the afternoon onwards Charly drank beer, something he never did in the shop.

He felt humiliated. He wondered what might have happened if he'd had a weapon rather than a camera with him.

"What would have happened if I'd had a weapon?"

"What sort of weapon?"

"A rifle. I could have done with a rifle. I'd have shot it dead."

She laughed.

"You don't have a rifle. Without a rifle you can't kill the wolf. Thank God."

"I'm going to get hold of one, I can get hold of one."

The boy and girl ran and crawled through the under-growth at the edge of the station complex. They saw the policemen's car and they saw the officers give up their search and go back inside the shed.

They ran to the large sliding gate and then in the dark-ness to Greifswalder Strasse. On the other side of the road they could see the neon lights of an Aldi supermarket.

At Aldi they bought things to eat: bread, cheese, salami and milk. And they bought vodka, rolling tobacco and cigarette papers.

"The vodka's for Icke," the boy said. "If he's there."

Icke was four years older than the two of them. He'd grown up in the same village. He and the boy had been friends, in spite of the difference in age – that wasn't important. At sixteen Icke had left school to start an apprenticeship as a locksmith, with blue-and-red-dyed hair and safety pins in his ears, and there had been a stabbing involving three skinheads at the bus station in Fürstenwalde, which Icke was lucky to survive. The knife had missed his artery by half a centimetre.

Icke came out of hospital with a big red scar on his neck,

he quitted his apprenticeship and went to Berlin. He moved into the apartment of an acquaintance at the end of Lychener Strasse.

It was a run-down block, but the apartment could be heated – if you could afford the coal.

The boy knew roughly where they were, Greifswalder Strasse, he remembered. He'd visited Icke for a fortnight last summer. They'd drunk a lot and smoked a lot of dope, while Icke had taken a few other substances, although the boy had not. Icke had told him to steer clear of those things. It would be a waste of a decent brain if something went wrong.

Icke had started writing all over the walls of his apartment. Not just the walls, but the doors too, the door frames, the window frames, the furniture. The boy didn't understand much of it, but the entire thing – or parts of it – read like a love poem or a lament. Icke often spoke of a girl, Maria, who he'd met by chance in Alexanderplatz. Maria had said he could move in with her in Lychener Strasse. She'd given him the key and he'd moved into the apartment, but Maria vanished and never came back. He never saw her again.

The apartment was her grandfather's, she had lived with him there. Then the old man had fallen ill. Maria looked after him day and night. During that time she started smoking heroin. The old man died and she continued to live there on her own.

Maria's father was Algerian and her hair was like wire. Icke had fallen in love with her, even though she was much older, and then she'd given him the key and said he could live there, but she never appeared again. Icke suspected she hadn't been able to cope and was probably dead.

He stayed in the flat, waiting for her. He stared at the railway trench in the sunset. He realised that no-one in this city was waiting for him, no-one had the slightest idea he was there. He began to write all over the walls.

Icke had changed in Berlin, but he was still something like a friend.

She hardly ever came here anymore, almost never in fact. He stood behind the counter in front of the meat spits: veal and chicken. The kebab shop at Kottbusser Tor belonged to him and his brother, he'd been running it for more than twenty years, but his daughter was studying and now she was starting work at a newspaper.

"Wolves?"

"Yes, tell me something about wolves."

Childhood memories. Anatolia. The mountains, the light just before sunset. Horse carts. Sheep, goats.

"Well, there's not much I can tell you about wolves." He laughed. "But now they've got one in Berlin."

He pointed at the television that hung below the ceiling in the corner of the takeaway.

"Just imagine." He drank tea. She drank coke. She was twenty-four. Made up, well dressed. He was very proud of her. *Kücüğüm.* My little one. *Güneşim*, my sunshine, the light of my eyes.

"I've only seen one once. Big. Really big. My uncle shot it. A huge beast."

There was nobody else in the kebab shop. He sat on a stool

behind the counter and behind him the meat spits, veal and chicken, rotated. By the window the bowls of tomatoes, salad, white cabbage and the sauces, yoghurt, herb or chilli.

"He came back to the village carrying the dead wolf across his shoulders, and we children believed it could still bite."

The boy and girl could have gone from Aldi back to Greifs-walder Strasse train station, but they thought it was too risky. They walked through the high-rise estate on Lilli-Henoch-Strasse until they came to Ernst-Thälmann-Park. At night-time in the snow the park was empty. They went to the planetarium. The park bordered the railway trench.

They arrived at Prenzlauer Allee station with their Aldi bags and the hunting rifle wrapped in blankets. They travelled just one station to Schönhauser Allee and during the journey he pointed to the left into the darkness beyond the window.

"Icke's apartment is somewhere there. You can see the rail-way from his apartment. They call it the trench, but he calls it the lakeside view."

The boy and girl got out at Schönhauser Allee. The streets were full of people, the pavements, the steps to the under-ground, which runs along Schönhauser Allee as an elevated railway on metal pillars. The boy and girl went under the rail-way towards Stargarder Strasse, and he told her about Icke.

A train passed over their heads.

He told her how he'd visited Icke in the summer, in the

holidays, how hot it had been, and how Icke had started writing all over the walls of the apartment because he was waiting for a girl.

She laughed. They were in good spirits. They went down Stargarder Strasse towards Lychener Strasse, passing Gethsemane Church. They stopped by shop windows. They turned left into a darker street, a dead end. The last house at the end of Lychener Strasse was covered in scaffolding, outside it were skips. They stopped in front of it.

"Nobody lives here," she said.

"Yes, Icke does."

"This is a building site," she said.

The entrance door was open. They went inside. On the ground floor the door to an apartment was ajar. They could hear noises. There was a stench coming from the apartment.

There wasn't a light in the stairwell, but they had lighters and matches. They went up the stairs. Beyond the second floor there were no more doors, just empty storeys. Everything had been gutted, all that remained were the load-bearing walls. They went up to the fourth floor, where Icke's apartment had been, but nothing was left of the apartment, no walls, no furniture. Plastic sheeting flapped in the windows.

"Are you sure we're in the right place?" she asked.

With their lighters burning they walked through the entire gutted fourth floor of the building. There was nothing here anymore, but then the boy spotted Icke's handwriting on one of the walls still standing.

They found a mat and a sleeping bag.

They sat on the mat, smoked and opened the bottle of vodka. They ate the things they'd bought and drank from the bottle, she drank quicker than he did.

Drunk now, they went down in the dark to the third floor and peed somewhere. Then they went back up, they still called it "Icke's apartment", they said, "Come on, let's go back to Icke's apartment," and then they carried on drinking as they stood by one of the empty window openings. They tore away the plastic sheeting and looked out at the railway tracks through the scaffolding.

"I think I might be getting ill," she said. "Let's go somewhere else, it's so cold here. We'll come back later."

The bottle of vodka was almost empty. They left the hunting rifle and beer there. In the darkness they went down the stairs. The door to the apartment on the ground floor was open. In the hallway stood a practically toothless old woman in a housecoat. She was holding a candle and seemed to be looking for something. She called out a name several times: Hansi. The girl knocked at the open door, but the woman didn't seem to hear her.

"Can I help you?" the girl asked. She was standing half inside the door. The apartment was warm, overheated, and the air was terrible.

The woman looked at her.

"Who are you?" she said, holding the candle higher.

"We're looking for someone," the girl said. "We've come to visit Icke."

"They cut off the electricity and water here. Only the stove works now."

The old woman looked at her, but said nothing more.

"Only the stove works now," she then repeated.

"The dog's disappeared," she said. "And my husband said that the dog jumped in the oven, but I don't believe that. He said the dog jumped in the oven because he couldn't stand the stench anymore. If we open the windows they'll rip them out," she said.

"Who?" the girl said.

"We burn our own shit, but I don't believe that. I don't believe that the dog leaped into the stove. He couldn't."

The woman looked at them for a moment longer before disappearing into a room off the hallway.

The girl stayed briefly in the doorway, warmed by the heat of the apartment and the vodka, the boy right behind her. They left the building. When they stepped out into the street snow was falling, mingled with scraps of burning paper that danced slowly in the air before landing on the road.

"If we get lost let's meet back here," the boy said.

The boy and girl stood at the end of the street in the light of a lamp, watching the burning paper fall slowly into the snow.

"What are you doing?" the girl called to the woman on the second-floor balcony of the house opposite.

"Burning my mother's diaries. She died," the woman on the balcony said.

"Looks beautiful," the girl said.

"And what are the two of you doing?" the woman asked.

"Looking for someone. Icke. Do you know Icke?"

"No," the woman said. "I don't know any Icke. No-one lives in that house anymore. They're gutting the entire thing. They're gutting everything around here."

"Yes," the girl said. "But there are still people living downstairs."

"Oh," the woman on the balcony said. "So where are you going now?"

"To look for Icke," the girl said.

"Now? Do you come from around here?" The blonde woman on the balcony kept lighting scraps of paper and throwing them into a metal bowl in front of her on the small balcony. The wind lifted the burning paper into the air and blew it into the street. The boy and girl saw the woman's face in the light of the fire beside her.

"No," the girl said. "We're not from here."

"Would you like to come up?"

"No," the girl said. "We want to find Icke," but the two of them stayed where they were, watching the bits of burning paper.

"Were you planning to stay the night at Icke's?"

"Yes," the girl said.

"Come up, then, you can sleep at my place. I've got room."

"No thanks," the girl said. "It's very kind, but we might still find him."

Tomasz got into the car and drove to the open-plan offices on Rosa-Luxemburg-Platz. It was just after seven o'clock, around the time Agnieszka would start cleaning in the offices. He called her, but she didn't answer. The floors that housed the offices were dark, he could see this from the street. She wasn't there. He drove on to their apartment in Neukölln, but he no longer had the key. He'd left the key there that morning. That morning he'd vowed never to return. There was no light on in the apartment and she still wasn't answering her phone. He rang the bell, but either she wasn't there or she wasn't opening up. He stood in the street, at a loss as to what to do. Even though it had stopped snowing it had turned colder. He considered driving back to Poland. He wondered whether he should wait all night here for her outside the house.

He drove back to the offices. He talked to her. He talked to her the whole time. He tried calling her, but she didn't answer and later her number was unavailable, switched off.

He sat in the car on Rosa-Luxemburg-Platz, looking up at the dark floors with the open-plan offices. He couldn't imagine that she wouldn't come to work. He waited two hours outside the building. He went to grab a bite to eat and when he came back the floors housing the offices were still dark. So long as he had something to do, so long as he had a goal he could keep his fear in check. The real fear, the huge fear arrived in idle moments. The fear that barely allowed him to open his eyes. He got back into the car and returned to Neukölln, but Agnieszka wasn't there, or she wasn't opening up.

It was half past ten. He called Agnieszka's best friend, Janina, who also lived in Berlin. Janina answered sleepily. She hadn't heard anything from Agnieszka, she said, not for days. She said he ought to go to bed, Agnieszka would come back, she'd come back for sure.

Late that afternoon Agnieszka had cleaned an apartment belonging to a family in Wörther Strasse on Kollwitzplatz, right beside the Jewish cemetery.

From their sitting room in winter, you could see the graves through the branches of the trees. In summer everything was green and you could only guess that the graves were there.

These people had children and sometimes she would look after them in the evenings. She liked the family.

Instead of going to the offices in Rosa-Luxemburg-Platz she took the underground to Moritzplatz in Kreuzberg. She walked down Oranienstrasse until she found the café. She didn't know the café, Andi had suggested it. They hadn't seen each other for five days.

Andi was already sitting in Café Lux when she came in. He was wearing a tracksuit. He smiled when he saw her. He had close-cropped blond hair. She liked his smile. "You could eat people up with your smile," she'd told him when they kissed for the first time.

He was sitting at a table by the window. Through the

window she could see that many people were out and about in Oranienstrasse.

Women in headscarves and long coats, students, punks, tourists, Turkish boys not wearing coats in spite of the cold, shouting to each other across the street.

"How did you find this place?" she said. "You don't live anywhere near here."

He watched the people in the street.

"I don't know," he said. "Here everything's very different from where I live. I could never live here."

"Why not?" she said.

He said nothing for a while, but looked at her as if there was something she hadn't understood.

"It's not my area," he said.

"What is your area?" she asked. "Why do you come here?"

"For that reason."

They couldn't go to his place because his mother was there.

Her mobile kept ringing. They went to her apartment in Neukölln. They didn't turn on any lights. Her mobile rang and she turned off the ringer, then switched it off altogether. Later the doorbell rang, but she didn't answer.

"I thought he'd go back to Poland," she said.

"Why?" he said. "I wouldn't go to Poland."

"But Poland's not your area either."

He gave a short laugh.

Later he said, "I don't want this child. No way."

"But what are we going to do?" she said.

"You're going to get rid of it. Lose it."

He made a gesture.

"But I can't," she said, "I'm a Catholic girl." She tried to sound funny.

"I don't care. There's no way I want this baby."

He was sitting beside her on the bed.

Fifteen minutes later Andi got dressed and left. She wanted to take a look out of the window first to see whether Tomasz was still waiting by the house, but Andi said it didn't matter.

"Listen, he doesn't know who I am. I could be anybody. He left the apartment. She heard him dart down the ten stairs to the entrance and then leave the house. The door clicked shut again. She went to the window to watch him, but he had already gone. Agnieszka locked her front door from the inside and left the key in the lock. She took a shower. She showered for half an hour and then went to bed. At around two o'clock her friend Janina sent her a text message. "Tomasz is here."

The regional train to Berlin was virtually empty. The boy's father got out at Berlin Hauptbahnhof. He'd never got out at Hauptbahnhof before, to him this was a new building. He found a payphone and called his brother. The man's brother lived in a small apartment in Dunckerstrasse.

His brother was at home.

"I'm here," he said.

The boy's father took the S-Bahn to Alexanderplatz and then the tram up Prenzlauer Allee. He got out and crossed Raumerstrasse, turning right into Dunckerstrasse, then passed Helmholtzplatz to get to his brother's apartment.

The boy's father rang the bell and heard his elder brother's voice over the intercom, which hadn't been there in the past. Back then, in the late eighties and early nineties, he and his brother had lived there together for a while, just after the wall came down, but then he went back. Many people were leaving the village at the time and he went back.

After the wall came down his brother spent a few years working as a lighting technician in the theatre, but then he started getting pains, problems with his back and spinal discs. He was signed off work for a long time, he was operated on, rehab, detoxification from all the painkillers, and at some point it became obvious that he wouldn't work again. That he would never work again.

The man's brother stood on the second floor and nodded. A man in his late fifties, tall, heavy, unemployed for years. An old man, the boy's father thought, with a drinker's face.

"The boy's run away," he said. "With a girl. They went on foot, then by train and now they're in Berlin."

The brother nodded.

"He's not here." He stood in the hall between the kitchen door and the entrance to the sitting room. A single lightbulb hung in the hallway.

"Fancy a drink?"

Music was playing on the kitchen radio and then someone said something about the wolf in Berlin. The man's brother shook his head. It was one of his old habits, shaking his head. They hadn't seen each other for several years.

"Run away," he said, shaking his head. "He's not here," the man said again. He was wearing slippers. The interior of the apartment hadn't changed in the last twenty years.

When they'd briefly lived here together, they'd taken off the door to the sitting room and mounted it beneath the ceiling in the hallway as a storage area. They'd called their construction "the attic". The "attic" was still there.

"He's not here," the man said for the third time, shaking his head. "Hungry?" Hungry.

They went into the small kitchen. Gloomy light everywhere, but above the little table in the kitchen was a bright, low-hanging lamp. On the table the man put a plate, bread and salami in a plastic pack. He hadn't had any visitors for a long while. Then he poured two glasses of schnapps. One he held in his hand, the other he placed on the table.

"So where is he then? Where are they? It's cold outside."

"They were at the freight station."

"Which freight station?"

"Greifswalder Strasse."

"Oh, just round the corner. I thought that didn't exist anymore. And?"

"Vanished."

"Cheers."

The man's brother raised his schnapps glass.

"Yes, cheers," the boy's father said, also raising his glass.

Pick me up at Neumann, there's a party going on here, her friend had said. "Neumann", a gallery in Auguststrasse. The girl's mother had got to the city just before eleven at night. She parked her car and walked to the gallery. Outside the gallery she stopped and stood in the darkness.

She'd been expecting a private view, a party, but in the cold fluorescent light of the gallery there were just a few people standing around, drinking sparkling wine from plastic cups.

She watched her friend through the window. Her friend was wearing a short skirt and red shoes, talking to a terribly vain-looking man with grey hair. The gallerist, perhaps, or the artist, the girl's mother thought. She recognised the man, but she could not say from where. The woman with the red shoes and the grey-haired man were laughing, through the window it looked as if they were flirting, and then the man and her friend suddenly went for each other – she slapped him in the face, he hit back and then she pulled his hair. The whole thing came as such a surprise and was over so quickly that no-one could intervene. Putting on her coat, her friend left the gallery and threw herself into her arms.

"What was that all about?" the girl's mother said.

"Nothing," her friend said. "He asked me if my sex life had changed since I'd been taking psychotropic drugs, and whether I'd sleep with him if he took some too and then we could turn it into a photographic exhibition."

The girl's mother said nothing. She remembered where she knew the man from. He had said something similar to her fifteen years ago, but she hadn't slapped him in the face. She had laughed.

He held the empty glass in his hand and smoked. He looked at his elder brother with his over-long, thin hair, as he gave him a third refill. He reckoned he still had everything under control. He felt in good shape and he saw everything very clearly. He knew that the following morning he would remember what they were talking about now. He was happy because he knew how the evening would pan out: they would talk more and more, he and his brother, with whom he'd only ever talked when both of them were drunk. They talked about work and the fact that they no longer had any, and whether or not they should have gone freelance and why they didn't. They didn't talk about their wives, not about his, nor about his brother's who'd left him a few years previously.

When the schnapps bottle was empty they put on their coats and walked the short distance to a kiosk that stayed open late and sold schnapps, beer, cigarettes, crisps and sweets.

The cold air did them good and the man told his brother about his search for the boy and girl in the woods, and the dead man by the hide and his night up in the hide.

The boy and girl walked down Lychener Strasse in search of a pub where the boy had been several times with Icke in the summer, but the boy couldn't remember exactly where the pub was. They walked the entire length of Lychener Strasse and crossed Danziger Strasse, although the boy was certain that it hadn't been so far from Icke's apartment to the pub, and then they continued southwards on Knaackstrasse past Kollwitzplatz. On the other side of Kollwitzplatz a group of drunk people were talking loudly by a kiosk.

They turned right into Kollwitzstrasse and kept heading south until the houses came to an end on one side of the street. In the darkness beyond a tall fence they could make out something like a hut, from which they heard noises, the clank of metal on metal.

"Sounds like a smithy," the girl said.

The boy seemed to remember this sound of metal on metal from the summer. Now he thought the pub might be somewhere near here after all.

Her friend lived in Prenzlauer Berg, at the very end of Schwedter Strasse, above the Gleimtunnel. From her apartment she had a view of a playground, a children's farm, a climbing wall and then across the railway to Wedding and Gesundbrunnen. In the past, when she was a student and afterwards, the two women had lived here together. At the time there was still a border, the wall still standing. The girl's mother had tasted her first success, she'd been "on the circuit", as she referred to it later: exhibitions, photo ops, interviews.

She was attractive and had a quick tongue. She stood for a young generation of eastern German women artists in re-unified Berlin, but it wasn't her work itself that was the focus of attention. It was her personality, her charisma. She had far more success than her friend, who lacked the talent to sell herself. Then she met the girl's father, a highly successful painter and sculptor, even back then. She moved out of the apartment above the Gleimtunnel with its sweeping view, she and the sculptor got married in a flash, she fell pregnant and almost simultaneously her career came to a standstill. For the first few years she couldn't understand what was happening.

She couldn't understand why interest in her work had waned. Then she began to blame it on her husband's success. She accused him of doing nothing for her.

Her friend had stayed in Schwedter Strasse the whole time. She didn't marry, didn't have any children – she was on her own most of the time. She took jobs to keep her head above water, for a while she got teaching contracts at her old art school, but it wasn't enough for a professorship – other people were given those. In the end she had no work at all. She tried to keep in touch with the art scene, but she found it increasingly difficult to keep smiling at the exhibition openings. She'd always had melancholy phases. When she turned forty she was forced to admit to herself that her artistic career had failed and that she had nothing in life, no family and no work. She plummeted into a deep depression.

She checked herself into a psychiatric clinic and stayed there for more than half a year. When eventually she left the clinic she knew that without work she wouldn't cope in the outside world for more than a couple of months. She asked at the children's farm opposite whether they might have anything for her. She said she was skilled in working with wood, stone, metal and clay. She was a sculptress, she could offer courses, but at the farm they were only looking for trained teachers or animal carers – that had been stipulated by the Berlin Senate. A month later she was on the verge of returning to the clinic. She asked at the farm again and this time they offered her hourly-paid work as a caretaker and cleaner. To begin with she found the work humiliating, but the regular contact with teachers and children stabilised her.

She began to draw again and went to the occasional exhibition opening. She didn't lie when she was asked what she did, not even on that evening in the gallery on Auguststrasse. She'd known the man with grey hair for years, and she knew his jokes too. Back when they were students she and her friend used to make fun of him, one of the first West Germans to study in the East in the early nineties. As an artist and a man they found him ludicrous, but he understood the market. Quicker than anyone he realised that he had no future as an artist himself, but he opened a gallery in Mitte which became a success and some of the artists he showed there were now selling their pictures all over the world. Art Basel. Miami. He wore suits – even as a student – and he didn't exhibit women artists, almost never.

The girl's mother stood in her old apartment looking at the drawings on the walls. The drawings were very simple. A horse, a goat, a second goat, a house.

"Where's that?" she asked.

"That's the farm," her friend said. "Down there, opposite our building. I work there now."

The girl's mother said nothing.

"Why did she run away?"

Her friend didn't look at her when she asked the question.

"I expect she couldn't bear living with me anymore."

"So why have you come after her?"

In front of the kiosk a few men and a young woman were standing beneath an awning, smoking.

The boy's father and his brother bought four litres of beer and two bottles of schnapps. The brother paid, he said he had money. It occurred to the boy's father that he'd forgotten to ring his wife again, but now it was too late anyway. They opened the first beer outside the kiosk. They stood with the others beneath the awning, smoking and looking out at the wet snow. The man's brother knew the owner of the kiosk by name, he called him Charly, and Charly knew the man's brother by name: Udo.

"And that's my brother, Walter," Udo said. "He's looking for his boy."

"Oh," Charly said. "I'll ask around. Where are you from?"

The boy's father said he came from near Beeskow, but Charly didn't know Beeskow, so the boy's father told him it wasn't far from Frankfurt an der Oder, and Charly said: "Wasn't the wolf there? That's where the wolf came from. From the east. Vierlinden bei Seelow."

"The wolf," the boy's father said. "Yes, the wolf was there, apparently. Seelow. That's further north."

"Not 'apparently', he *was* there. Come on, you're from Beeskow, please don't tell me you're one of those people who doesn't believe the wolf exists, because it does, I saw it with my own eyes."

"I'm not saying the wolf doesn't exist, I'm just saying I haven't seen it."

"I have!" Charly said, or almost shouted, opening his eyes wide, "and what if, what if . . ."

"Charlie," Jacky said, "your eyes are like saucers again – and you're talking very loudly."

"But Jacky," Charly said, "you know it's true, if anyone knows it's true, it's you."

"You saw it?" the man's brother said.

"I saw it, Udo, it was standing in front of me."

"Where?" Udo said.

"He saw it," Jacky said.

"It was standing in front of me," Charly said, "and if only I'd taken a picture of it, but I couldn't, I couldn't do it. But it was standing there in front of me."

"Charly," Jacky said.

"I didn't see it standing in front of me," the boy's father said, "but I was in the woods and I saw tracks."

"Tracks?" Charly's eyes opened wide. "You saw wolf tracks, that means it was nearby, it must have been close, where was that?"

"In the woods, I don't know where."

"You could have shot it."

"I couldn't shoot it."

"But you might have shot it."

"Charly, it's time to close up," Jacky said.

"Wait, wait, wait, this man saw the wolf."

"He didn't see it."

"I didn't see it."

"Tell me what the tracks looked like, what do wolves' tracks look like?"

"Do you want to go wolf hunting?" the man's brother said. "Do you want to hunt the wolf? Well, you can. The wolf's in Berlin, you need to go up to Gesundbrunnen, it was spotted there today."

"Yes, yes, yes, I'll find it, I'll shoot it, I'll go up to Gesundbrunnen."

"You're not allowed to shoot it," the man's brother said. "You can hunt it down, but you can't shoot it dead."

"All I need is a weapon, give me a weapon and I'll shoot it. That animal humiliated me."

"Come on, Charly," Jacky said, "we're closing." They drank up their beer.

The two men made their way back to Dunckerstrasse. They didn't talk anymore about the wolf. They talked about things that the boy's father could not remember later, but they talked a lot. In the apartment they kept drinking, alternating between schnapps and beer. They sat opposite one another at the small kitchen table and smoked, then they talked about their parents, their childhood and adolescence in the countryside near the Polish border, and to the boy's father, who was now very drunk, this seemed to have been a particularly happy time.

"Like a lost diamond," he said, and his brother didn't understand what he meant because he'd just been talking about something completely different, so he shook his head. And then the boy's father was struck by something, a vague memory or feeling, he became melancholic, tears welled in his eyes, and with the melancholy came a despair that rocked him. He lit a cigarette and kept drinking schnapps.

Tomasz rang the bell at Janina's in Wedding. It was just after two in the morning. He couldn't stand it anymore. He'd spent the whole evening driving back and forth from the offices on Rosa-Luxemburg-Platz to Agnieszka's apartment. She hadn't opened the door to him, she wasn't at the offices and he couldn't call her.

In the end he'd parked somewhere and sat in the car in the cold, but then he was seized by panic again. Shortness of breath, cold sweats, racing heart.

He'd got out and gone into a pub, outside which a lot of young people were smoking. Loud music was playing inside and people were dancing. He felt as if they were staring at him in his work clothes. A girl with dyed-blonde hair had asked him where he came from, but he hadn't understood her and then the girl and her friend had laughed.

"A Russian." They laughed and clinked their glasses with him. "You must be a Russian." And he replied in Polish that he wasn't Russian, but the girls didn't understand even though it wasn't difficult to understand.

Once again he felt he couldn't breathe properly so he left

the pub, got into his car and drove to Janina's.

Janina opened the door wearing only knickers and a T-shirt. Behind her stood her boyfriend, Krzysztof. Tomasz knew him too.

"You can sleep on the sofa," Janina said. "Or you can watch the telly."

The tipsy girl, who usually said little, was suddenly very talkative as they walked through the streets of Berlin in the snow.

"It's like a grid," she said, "everything's like a grid."

"What, the city?"

"No, everything. It seems as if there's nothing but straight lines, all paths are set out, you can't deviate from the grid, like on a canal or when you're walking along cracks and you can't change direction until you get to the end of a paving stone and the next one begins."

The boy and girl got their bearings from the television tower and kept heading south, towards Mitte, they walked along Schönhauser Allee until the boy stopped outside a place with black windows.

The pub had no name. It was painted black all over. A dark-haired woman and a blonde woman were working behind the bar. The dark-haired one was talking to a man. Apart from his odd brief comment or question, she was the one doing the talking. He had an accent and looked as if he came from South America.

The waitress talked and talked, smoked, took a sip of beer and went on talking. The South American listened, occasionally turning to glance at the other people in the pub. He nodded to the boy as if he knew him, but the boy didn't recognise the man.

The blonde waitress put two vodkas and two beers on the bar for the girl and boy. The dark-haired woman was talking about men and women and sex, saying that really she was only attracted to women, then the blonde one gave her a slap on the bum. They laughed and the South American laughed too.

The boy and girl sat by a wall, almost vanishing entirely in the black pub. All that was visible in the darkness were their pale faces.

"Have you been here before?" the girl said, but he shook his head.

In the warmth the two of them soon grew tired. He asked the blonde waitress for two more beers. The dark-haired waitress was still talking to the South American and the South American occasionally turned to glance at the other people in the pub. A telephone rang. The dark-haired waitress passed the receiver to the South American, he spoke Arabic.

In spite of the music the boy and girl both fell asleep. The blonde waitress shook the boy awake and asked if everything was alright.

"Everything's fine," he said.

She said he ought to look her in the eye, then she let the two of them sleep.

It was half past one in the morning when the girl's mother and her friend heard the noise. It sounded like a scream or a whine. The friend was worried that something might have happened at the farm, "I've never heard anything like that."

As they headed across to the stable on the farm they heard the noise again.

"Maybe it's a cat," the girl's mother said.

"Maybe it's something else," her friend said.

To begin with in the darkness they couldn't find the lock to the stable door. Eventually they opened up, switched on the light and locked the door behind them. They walked through the stable, inspecting each pen with large torches. A few goats, two ponies. Six sheep. Chickens. Everything was quiet. The woman's friend checked the large door that led to the enclosures and the meadow.

"We need a guard."

"Why?"

"A wolf was seen here, really near."

"But no wolf could get in here."

"Who knows?"

"Don't you have a dog here?"

They did have a dog on the farm, but the dog wasn't there. It wasn't on its chain.

At night on the roundabout in the playground next door young people would sit around in the snow, drinking beer. The girls would sometimes shriek, but that wasn't the noise they'd heard.

The two women went with their torches to check the rest of the farm. Just as they were locking the stable door they heard the noise again. It was coming from the railway trench. The women shone their torches into the darkness but they couldn't see anything.

"What do you do with the animals?" the girl's mother said.

"Nothing," her friend said. "We keep them. That's all. The children look after them."

When the girl awoke briefly, the dark-haired waitress and the man were sitting at a table beside them, kissing passionately. He'd pulled up her T-shirt, she wasn't wearing anything underneath. The blonde waitress stood behind the bar, smoking and watching them. Then a glass smashed.

When the girl woke again later on, the blonde woman was no longer there. The pub was empty. Outside it was beginning to get light.

The girl sat there without moving. The boy was asleep.

The man was standing back at the bar, the dark-haired woman beside him.

The boy woke up.

"Where now?" he said.

They paid at the bar.

"Do you know anyone called Icke?" the boy asked.

"No," the woman said, looking at the man. The man shook his head.

"We're looking for work," the girl said.

It was three o'clock in the morning when the woman on the balcony in Lychener Strasse stopped burning her mother's diaries. She was standing in her coat and scarf on the small balcony of her apartment. The two children hadn't come back.

Then down below, where Lychener Strasse ended abruptly with a fence, she saw a large dog or, as it seemed to her, a wolf.

Tomasz sat in the dark on the sofa in Janina's apartment. He stared at the television, but didn't switch it on. Janina and Krzysztof were asleep in the room next door. Tomasz stayed in the apartment for just under an hour, then got up. He left without saying goodbye to Janina and Krzysztof. He walked to his car then drove back to the building site in Lychener Strasse.

In the dark Tomasz walked up the four floors of the house and turned on the floodlight upstairs. He stopped dead. Beside his rucksack he found ripped-open packets and wrappers, an almost-empty bottle of vodka and a hunting rifle.

He spent a long time looking at the rifle before picking it up. In the light of the lamp, Tomasz stood amongst the rubble on the gutted floor and held the hunting rifle in his hands. He raised the rifle and aimed at the vodka bottle, but didn't shoot.

He crawled into his sleeping bag, leaned against the wall and placed the rifle beside him. He listened. Silence in the building. He listened out for the owners of the rifle to come back, they had to come back. But nobody did. The rifle lay beside him. Tomasz slept for a few minutes, woke up, fell asleep again and then was startled from his sleep by a noise. It was getting light. An old woman with practically no teeth was standing amongst the rubble, saying over and over again: "He isn't here. He isn't here." The woman didn't see him. She was wearing a housecoat. She was thin, emaciated. The old woman stood there for a while, then left. Tomasz could hear her footsteps on the stairs.

He dreamed that the wolf was standing before him in the rubble. The wolf was standing in the middle of the empty floor, in his dream Tomasz raised the rifle several times and then he woke up.

Outside it was light. In the street the girl and boy stood in the snow together with the waitress and the South American. They'd told the waitress and the South American about their hike through the woods, their journey on the freight train to Berlin, and the man, a Chilean, said they could come with him. He said they could stay with him for a few days, he had enough room. The Chilean was called Yuri, like Yuri Gagarin, the cosmonaut, the first man in space, son of a carpenter and a milkmaid.

"My father was a communist," Yuri said. "You can work here," he told the girl. "You can't work for me," he told the boy, "I don't need two new people, but you can both stay with me, I've got enough room for everyone."

The Chilean, the waitress, the boy and the girl walked up Schönhauser Allee. The Chilean was in his late forties or early fifties.

"Have you heard about the wolf?" the Chilean said. "Now there's a wolf in Berlin, a wolf in Wedding, but before that it was in Marzahn, do you know where that is? No, you don't, and now the wolf is in Wedding and I'm wondering when someone's going to shoot the wolf," and the Chilean lifted up his arms as if he were holding a rifle. "I wouldn't shoot it, but then I don't have a rifle, I can't shoot it." He laughed. "I've only got a knife," and he pulled a large hunting knife from his long, grey-black coat before putting it straight back again. "I could only skin it."

They went on their way through the snow.

"That's exactly what you need," the waitress said.

"What?" the Chilean said. "What do I need?"

"A wolfskin."

"You're children, you know that?" the Chilean said. "And one thing *I* know is that children don't belong on the streets."

At half past seven the following morning, and without having had breakfast, the girl's mother drove to Dahlem.

The snow briefly turned to rain and then back to snow again. She had her ex-husband's address, but she'd never been there. A few years ago he'd bought a Bauhaus villa in southwest Berlin.

She only knew about her ex-husband's new house from what her daughter had told her, having been there twice. She'd never met his new wife either, even though he and the woman had been together for a long time now. Over the last few years there had been virtually no contact between her and the girl's father.

She drove to Dahlem without ringing ahead. It took her longer than she'd expected to find the house.

It was just after eight o'clock when she rang the bell. A young woman in a T-shirt and tracksuit bottoms and with an eastern European accent opened the door. At first the girl's mother thought it was her husband's new wife. The young woman told her that nobody was at home.

The girl's mother said that she was the man's ex-wife.

The young woman told her again that nobody was at home.

"Do you know when anyone will be back?"

"I can't say," Agnieszka said. "I don't know. They're not here."

"Is my daughter not here?"

"Nobody's here," Agnieszka said.

"Can I wait here until someone gets back?" the woman said.

Agnieszka showed the woman into the large white kitchen where the photographs were still hanging on the walls.

"I'm the cleaner," Agnieszka said, smiling briefly when she saw the woman looking at the photographs on the wall.

The girl's mother sat in the unfamiliar house, in the immaculately tidy, empty white kitchen. In front of her was a glass of water. Through the large windows she could see into the garden. The young woman had left her alone. At one point the girl's mother heard the young woman's voice coming from somewhere in the house, probably on the telephone to her ex-husband, and after that it was completely quiet. She couldn't hear anything, no vacuum cleaner, no radio.

In the photograph on the wall her ex-husband had long grey hair. Glasses, beard, a heavy man with a cigarette in one hand and a glass of red wine in the other. In the picture beside it was his wife, a Japanese woman, early forties. The third photograph was of the young woman who'd let her in, standing by the fridge in grey tracksuit bottoms and a baggy T-shirt. The pictures had been taken here in the kitchen.

The girl's mother sat for an hour at the long, chunky kitchen table. She hadn't called her ex-husband, the girl's father, when the girl ran away. He knew nothing about it – assuming the girl hadn't called him either.

She stood up, went to the large panes of glass and looked out into the garden. In the snow stood one of his works made of steel.

His steel sculptures, his cast works had always infuriated her. She'd always thought he was a painter, not a sculptor, and yet his sculptures sold as well as his pictures.

Shining steel. Expensive, extravagant, incredibly heavy. Flawless surfaces that time couldn't touch, as smooth as a mirror and completely empty.

She thought about leaving a note for him on the table, but decided against it. She went out of the kitchen, called "Goodbye!" into the silence and left the unfamiliar house.

The Chilean's apartment was in the basement. It was enormous, an entire vault measuring more than 250 square metres. Through the windows that gave onto the street you could see the legs of passers-by, but there weren't many people about yet.

Arabian carpets everywhere, even in the kitchen.

"Come in," the Chilean said. "I hardly ever have visitors. Hospitality is sacred to the Arabs."

He said something in a foreign language.

"That's Arabic. Welcome. Are you hungry? Let's have something to eat."

"How come you speak Arabic?" the girl said.

"I learned it," he said. "I've done a lot of travelling."

They sat on cushions around a large tray and ate, then the Chilean gave them blankets and showed them where they could sleep. He showed them the washing machine and the enormous bath.

"My hammam," the Chilean said, but the boy and girl didn't know what a hammam was.

"See you this evening," he said to the girl, "if not before."

The boy and girl slept until three in the afternoon. When they woke up the Chilean had gone.

"Let's get out of here," the boy said.

"No," the girl said.

"Let's get away from here. We'll find something else."

"No," the girl said.

Tomasz woke up in the cold. He felt as if he hadn't slept, but at some point he'd fallen asleep and dreamed about the wolf. He got up and left the gutted building. He threw his things and the rifle onto the back seat of the Toyota and drove to the villa in Dahlem where Agnieszka worked every morning.

He didn't ring the bell. He stood on the other side of the street and waited. He saw Agnieszka briefly at a window on the first floor. He waved at her, but she didn't see him. Later a woman with red hair came out of the house. The woman turned on the threshold and shouted something back into the house, but he couldn't hear what she said. Tomasz stood outside the house for three hours. He didn't ring the bell and didn't call her mobile. Then the door opened and Agnieszka came outside.

Tomasz and Agnieszka stood on the pavement on the other side of the street from the villa. They stood facing each other. She didn't say anything. She just looked at him.

"Come with me," he said.

"I'm not finished here," she said. "I arrived late."

"How much longer do you have to work?"

"Another hour."

"I'll wait then. I'll wait here."

She went back into the house, turned and looked at him and was about to say something, but didn't.

"I'll wait here," he said. She nodded and went back into the villa. Agnieszka didn't have anything more to do there, she'd finished a while ago. She walked through the empty house and then sat in the kitchen. She looked at the photographs on the wall and then through the windows into the garden.

The girl's mother left the district with its villas in the south-west of the city and drove east again. Her fury returned, this time with a vengeance, she screamed so loudly and violently in her car that it hurt.

She stopped in a side street outside the entrance to a former brewery in Prenzlauer Berg. She walked across the cobbled courtyard to the workshop, the studio. She knew the place from before. In spite of the cold, the heavy iron sliding gate was half open. He was wearing black overalls and stood with his back to the courtyard. He was welding. Music was playing. She called his name, his surname, she'd always called him by his surname.

The girl's father switched off the flame, flipped up his welding mask and turned towards the courtyard. They hadn't seen each other for a few years.

"What's happened?" he said.

"She's run away," she said. She tried to smile.

He looked at her and said nothing.

"When?" he said at last.

"Four days ago," she said.

He was even heavier, bulkier than the last time they'd met. Tall and heavy. As she looked at him, she thought: He hates me and he's right to.

"Why didn't you call me?" he said.

"I thought she might be with you."

"She's not with me. If she'd been with me I would have called you."

She didn't say anything. She stood in the courtyard in the snow, pulling on her cigarette.

"Have you spoken to the police?"

She nodded.

In the darkness of the workshop behind him she couldn't quite make out what he was working on.

What she could make out reminded her of the ribs of a whale.

"She didn't run away on her own. There's a boy with her. The boy from the village. They're in Berlin."

"How do you know?"

"They were seen together at a freight station. At Greifs-walder—"

"At the cement works?"

She shrugged. She was from the east of the city, but she didn't know the cement works.

"When was that?"

"Yesterday."

He said nothing more. They didn't have anything else to say to each other. He slid the iron gate further open. The workshop – or the studio – was vast. She saw his car, the old car he'd always had.

"What now?" she said.

"I'm going to look for her," he said.

"But you've no idea what she looks like," she said.

He said: "I do know what she looks like."

"Where?" she said.

"Where what?"

"Where are you going to look for her?"

"No idea."

He got into the car and reversed out of the workshop. Then he got out and walked past her to the iron gate. He was wearing heavy lace-up boots with steel caps, the same shoes he'd worn twenty years earlier. He called out a name and said something in a language she didn't understand.

His assistant. Or his new wife. The girl had told her about the new wife. He had a liking for foreign assistants and foreign women, he'd had it before her and after her, and in the past she'd wondered whether as an East Berliner she had also been something of a foreign woman for him.

He slid the heavy gate until it was about half a metre open and then drove off without another word.

After fifty minutes Agnieszka stood up in the kitchen of the villa in Dahlem, went to the door, put on her coat and left the house.

Tomasz smiled at her as she came over to him.

"Everything's going to be fine," he said twice on the way to the car. Agnieszka was amazed, she'd never heard him say anything like that before. He never usually spoke like that.

She didn't see the rifle until she was already in the car.

"What are you doing?" she said. "Are you going to kill me? Where did you get that rifle?"

"I found it."

"Found it?"

"At the building site."

He drove off. She started to panic.

"Are you going to kill me?" she screamed. "Are you going to kill me?"

"No," he said, trying to calm her down, but at the same time reluctant to stop the car in case she got out and ran away. "No, I'm not going to kill you, I just found the rifle at the building site."

"How can you find a rifle at the building site? Nobody finds rifles at building sites," she screamed.

"I did find it . . ."

She reached behind her to grab the rifle. She wanted to throw it out of the car, but the rifle was too long, it got wedged. While driving he made a grab for the rifle too. The barrel was pointing at him. With one hand she was holding the rifle, with the other she opened the door of the moving car. She screamed and screamed and pulled the rifle and then a shot was fired. The bullet grazed Tomasz's forehead. The window on the driver's side shattered. He managed to bring the car to a stop, but he was bleeding heavily, his entire face was covered in blood and he screamed in pain or fright. She screamed too and then he screamed again that he *had* just found the rifle, just found it, and she screamed: "What are we going to do now? What are we going to do now? You've got to go to hospital, you've got to go to hospital."

He screamed: "Why did you do that?" And she screamed: "I didn't mean to, I didn't mean to."

He held his bloody forehead. Blood was streaming into his eyes. He got out and was almost knocked down by a car that was trying to overtake the Toyota in the middle of the road. She got out too, but first she threw the rifle onto the back seat. He said: "Drive me to hospital."

"Which hospital? I don't know a hospital."

"Just take me to any hospital."

She drove off. He sat beside her, bleeding and occasionally

groaning. She did not know where to go. The window was broken. It was freezing cold and as she drove the snow flew into her face.

Zeynep and she had once been best friends. Zeynep had found a job in a beauty salon and now they were sitting in the ice-cream parlour in Gesundbrunnen shopping centre. Zeynep said, "What have you got to do with the wolf?"

"Nothing," the young woman said, "but I'm writing about it."

"What? What do you mean you're writing?"

Zeynep knew her friend's tendency to exaggerate, but she also knew she'd finished school, got her leaver's certificate, studied, was working for a newspaper, everything was possible.

The two young women ate huge, colourful ice-cream sundaes with complicated names, and both knew at that moment that they had nothing in common except for a period in their childhood or adolescence – and a shared language, which sometimes appeared for a few words or partial phrases, then vanished again and reappeared, *arada sirada*, even though the country in which this language was spoken was a long way from the country in which they lived and had been born.

The people in the busy shopping centre. Escalators. Music.

"Right then, you and the wolf."

Zeynep laughed.

"You and the wolf."

"Me and the wolf, and the wolf and I."

"I've got to get back, my break's over."

"I know."

"Best of luck, then. Come by again sometime. How are your parents, by the way?"

"They're fine. How about yours?"

"They're fine too."

"And what do they say about the wolf?"

The young woman shrugged.

"Nothing. Well . . . my dad says he once saw a wolf when he was a child, but it was already dead."

"How big are wolves?"

"No idea."

The young woman laughed.

"Don't you know?"

"I really don't know."

The girl's father drove to Greifswalder Strasse. His mobile rang.

"We could look together. She's the daughter of both of us, after all."

"I don't want to look for her with you."

"Why not? She's the daughter of both of us, after all."

"Yes, but I don't want to. I'm scared of your angry outbursts."

"If you're so scared, how could you have left your daughter with me all these years?"

The girl's father was considerably older than his ex-wife. A tall man, overweight. A giant. He was a well-known painter and sculptor, worldwide.

The man went looking for his daughter in the city, but couldn't find her. Berlin has three and a half million inhabitants. He knew how pointless it was to go looking for her, but he set out to all the same. He drove around the city. He drove and drove, all the while aware of how pointless it was. He knew he would have to wait until she came to him and he knew she wouldn't come. The girl's father drove up Greifswalder Strasse, to the cement works, to the freight station, and there he spoke with the policemen, but these weren't the same policemen who'd been given the slip by the children the evening before. He asked when the men would be back on duty and what their names were, and he was told they couldn't give him any information, so the girl's father asked how it could have happened, how something like that could have happened, and then the girl's father blew his top.

He stood outside the transport police shed and screamed and screamed, he completely lost it, and the police officers, who were both fat men, said, "Come on now," and later said, "you've made your point," and then they said, "you really have made your point," and then they said, "that's quite enough now."

The girl's father guessed that the children had no money. He looked for them in Görlitzer Park. He looked for them on the pedestrian bridge beneath the railway tracks at Schiffbauer Damm, where a man stood selling a street newspaper, singing "Two little angels, flying far away", over and over.

He looked for them in Alexanderplatz, he looked for them in Mauerpark, then he looked for them at Gleisdreieck, he drove up and down Oranienstrasse, and finally he looked for them in Wrangelkiez, Kreuzberg.

"How did it happen?" the doctor at the hospital said, but Tomasz didn't understand the question and Agnieszka was standing outside in the corridor of the casualty department.

"How did it happen?" the man said again with a questioning gesture.

"Accident," Tomasz said.

"You've got to stay here. Here. In hospital."

"No," Tomasz said. "I can't stay here. I must go to Poland. With my wife."

Agnieszka stood waiting in the green-and-white hospital corridor.

An old woman with a plastic bag walked past her, stopped and gazed at her.

"My, you're a beautiful child."

"I'm sorry?"

"All the things that have happened to me."

"Really? What happened?"

"Three horses."

The woman walked on a few paces, stopped again and turned back to Agnieszka.

"And three men."

"Three men?"

"I was twenty-two when the war was over. They threw the piano out of the window. And they shot the horses."

"What happened to the men?"

"Well, then, goodnight and goodbye."

"Goodbye."

The girl's mother sat at Brunnenstrasse police station at the corner of Invalidenstrasse. She'd always hated this building from the outside, and now she was sitting inside it. It seemed to her as if the interior of the building was nothing but the exterior turned inside out, the other side of a recently skinned hide, and it smelled like it too.

"Have you got animals in here?" she said, and the policeman didn't reply.

"What happens now?" she said a little later.

"Now," the policeman said. "Now . . ."

It was as if he'd been fearing this question, as if he'd long been prepared for it.

"Now we wait."

The house had three rooms. The sitting room and a bedroom below, and another room on the first floor. Once upon a time the house had belonged to a manor, one of many workers' houses. The manor house itself had been turned into a children's home after the war, and now it had been up for sale for years. It was crumbling. The girl's parents, the artists from Berlin, had bought the old village schoolhouse. It stood opposite the workers' houses on the other side of the pond.

The woman had lived inside this house when she was a girl and later, after her parents died, lived there again with her husband and the boy.

The woman sat staring out of the window for almost the entire day. Sometimes she looked over to the other side of the village pond. The girl's mother had driven off a few days earlier, that night when the children had been stopped at the station. She'd heard the car.

The radio was on. The television was on. The woman was alone. She'd always wondered how someone could possibly buy an old schoolhouse. That such a thing was allowed.

She'd had the boy late. She was now in her early fifties, just a few years older than the girl's mother, but she looked considerably older.

They'd never spoken to each other. It was as if they weren't able to. It didn't work. Whenever they tried, even briefly, it led to misunderstandings. No matter whether they were discussing mildew or aphids. Or something she needed from town but couldn't buy because she didn't have a car.

The boy's mother couldn't explain *why* it was like this, all she knew was that it was so.

She sat beside the telephone. Since he'd gone to Berlin her husband hadn't called again. The woman knew what that meant. She could have called her husband's brother, but she didn't because it would have been pointless.

Since the episode at the freight station she'd heard nothing more of the children – or from the police. The children. She'd always liked the girl. The woman had called the girl "my sunshine".

The girl's mother hadn't said goodbye when she left that evening. She hadn't said anything.

The radio was on. On the radio they said that they were trying to capture the wolf, but they would shoot it if there were no other option.

They said there had been wolves not so long ago, which had migrated thousands of kilometres to start new packs. As far away as Russia.

They said there was something not quite right about the wolf. Wolves usually shied away from humans, cities. Unlike foxes these days. Foxes in Berlin – the boy's mother had not known that.

On the kitchen table was the girl's mother's telephone number, she'd had it for a few years. But the woman didn't know what to say to her. Or what to ask.

Music.

Discussion. Rabies could be ruled out. No, rabies couldn't be ruled out. Rabies could definitely be ruled out. How could it definitely be ruled out?

Perhaps it wasn't a wolf, but a dog. Yes it was, you could tell by the tracks. Wolves move in a straight line, dogs don't – what does that mean? – how are we to interpret that? She switched off the radio. The cawing of winter birds. The boy's mother switched on the radio again.

"I'm going to find it."

Charly opened his eyes wide.

"Charly—"

"I'm going to find it, Jacky, I'm going to find it again, I found it yesterday, I know where to find it, I'm going to find it again today."

"Why do you want to find it, Charly? Leave it alone."

He looked at her.

"No," he said. "No."

In the kiosk Charly had put up a map of the city, and on the map he'd marked the places where the wolf had been seen or supposedly seen.

"I'm going to find it."

The wolf had moved from Marzahn towards Wedding, the evening before he'd been seen in the railway trench near Bösebrücke, from the trains a succession of tired commuters had taken photographs of the wolf in the twilight, even though you could see virtually nothing in the pictures, but how had the wolf got from Marzahn to Wedding? On the news they said that someone had seen the wolf's tracks at the northern end of Mauerpark, last night, near the children's zoo. And then apparently the wolf was spotted in Hasenheide, in Kreuzberg and on the runway at Tempelhof Airport, but that was impossible. They must have been dogs.

The map on the wall of the kiosk was covered with markings, drawing pins, arrows, and each hour there were more of them. Charly tried to identify a pattern in the wolf's movements, but there was no pattern.

"How about using some bait?"

The comment came from a customer, someone, an old man. "In fishing we call it 'chumming'."

Charly opened his eyes wide.

"But bait without a hook?"

Charly had begun to ask around. He asked the regulars in his shop whether they knew anyone who had a rifle. Some said they would keep their ear to the ground, and then one of the customers did in fact come back with the telephone number of a man in Hofbrechtsfelde, a village a few kilometres north of Berlin, who might have a pistol for sale.

In the afternoon the girl's mother was back in the apartment she'd once shared with her friend – the apartment above the Gleimtunnel.

The girl's mother stood at the window, looking down at the children's farm. Her friend was down there in the slush with two goats. She waved up at the window. The girl's mother waved back. She thought about going down, but didn't. She stayed at the window, watching her friend talk to two children, two girls in colourful winter coats.

She thought about her house in the village. She thought about a wooden sculpture that was slowly rotting in her garden, an aeroplane. The girl had loved playing on it. This memory pained the woman, it pained her more than anything else that had happened in the past. She stood at the window and bit her finger.

The telephone rang. It was beside the woman, on the kitchen table. It was the bus driver, the ex-husband of her sister who now lived in Brunswick. Every day at half past six in the morning the bus driver pulled up at the bus stop, stopped, opened the door, even though nobody got on or off, closed the door. Drove on. He asked how the woman was. "Oh, you know," she said. That's how life is in the country.

The front door was open, there was no bell to ring, or not anymore. He walked up the old stairs, a dark, broad stairwell, no light, old stickers on the doors.

The parquet. The long hallway, the five-metre-high ceilings, the mouldings. Two hundred and fifty square metres, large rooms. A towering old tiled stove, a hundred and fifty years old, or even older. The hole in one of the walls. They'd called the apartment the paper palace, because the best thing about it was the fact that there was no rent, the apartment belonged to her. Her father, who they called the Nazi, owned a number of paper factories and he'd bought the apartment and given it to his daughter for her eighteenth birthday, two hundred and fifty square metres, with a view of the river, the Spree, Happy Birthday. Six of them had lived here together, sometimes ten or fifteen. People moved in and out, people she hardly knew and with whom she spent nights talking, drinking, smoking, and who vanished as suddenly as they'd arrived, never to be seen again – and then someone had leaped out of the window because he thought he could fly. Mushrooms. These days she lived here alone.

He knocked, she opened the door, they hadn't seen each other in thirty-five years, and she laughed and said: "Oh my God!"

She didn't invite him in, she simply walked or hopped down the long hallway, exclaiming, "Oh my God, oh my God, oh my God!" time and again, and then she turned to him and said, "Oh shit, oh shit, I still owe you money," and she laughed again. She was dressed like a girl. Both of them were thirty-five years older, but she behaved as if barely a day had passed. It's better that way, he thought. And then she said: "What are you wearing?" When he didn't answer she said: "I read about you in the paper sometimes. I always knew you'd be someone one day." Then she said, "What's wrong?"

He said: "My daughter's run away." She clapped her hands together in front of her face and he didn't know if this was a serious gesture or not, and she said: "But we did that too, we did exactly that."

"But not in winter," he said.

That evening the girl started work at the black-painted pub in Schönhauser Allee. She worked from seven in the evening until five in the morning. The boy sat in the corner of the pub and watched her work. At half past one the Chilean arrived, he went behind the bar and put his arms around the two waitresses.

At five o'clock they shut up shop. Again the four of them walked through the snow. Again they went to the Chilean's enormous basement apartment and, as they had the night before, sat around the tray, smoking.

From time to time the Chilean caressed the waitress and when he was talking occasionally he caressed the girl too, briefly, incidentally. He spoke about the city he came from: Valparaíso. He spoke about the Chilean forest, he spoke about the Andes. He said he'd spent ten years at sea. On a map of the world he showed them all the places he had been. Most of his time at sea, he said, had been spent below decks, in the engine room, then he had left the ship in Lebanon, in the port of Beirut.

"And I haven't set foot on a boat since."

"How many people have you told this story to?" the boy said.

"Stories are stories."

The Chilean paused.

"If you don't like me, you don't have to stay here," the Chilean said, smiling. "You're welcome to stay. But you don't have to."

"What's wrong with you?" the girl said to him later, as they were about to go to sleep.

"I don't believe him," the boy said.

Charly called the man. The following morning he made the trip out there. Friday morning, a beautiful winter's day, blue sky, very cold.

The man's house wasn't hard to find. Hobrechtsfelde was nothing more than a few houses and a few prefabricated buildings that stood empty. The man who opened the door was in his late seventies or early eighties. He was very thin. The man showed him the pistol.

"The Russians had pistols like this. Later they had the Makarov, but in the war they had this one, the Tokarev. The TT-33."

"How did you get hold of the gun?" Charly said.

"Do you want to try it out?"

The gaunt man went behind the house with Charly.

"Have you ever been here? Do you know what that is?" the man said. He pointed at the meadow behind the house. "That used to be a sewage farm. This is where all the effluent from the city trickled away for more than a hundred years. I've been living here for sixty years. Everything's contaminated. The soil here is completely contaminated."

He showed Charly how the pistol worked.

"Try it out. Have you ever fired a pistol before? It's best to use two hands."

Bauhaus. He didn't like the villa. He didn't like the area, the quiet. The street. The patches of snow under the trees. It was just after six o'clock.

When the girl's father wandered into the kitchen of the villa, his wife told him that the cleaner hadn't come.

The only things he liked about the house were the kitchen and the rockery built by his wife, who he'd been with for thirteen years – the wife who came after the girl's mother. He loved this wife.

The house belonged to him, but he had nothing to do with it, it had never been his house. Something about it wasn't right, something was wrong.

The man nodded, but said nothing. He drank coffee and imagined the large kitchen windows falling out of the wall.

The girl's father had barely slept a wink that night, worrying about the child, his daughter. He was going crazy with worry for his child, and he wondered how in spite of this it was possible to go on breathing. Last night he'd put this question to his wife, and in fact it wasn't possible, for a moment he hadn't been able to breathe, or at least he'd thought he couldn't, and then his wife had put her arms around him and eventually he'd fallen asleep. A couple of hours later he was awake again and knew that everything was wrong. Everything was wrong, it had been for years, all of a sudden he realised it, but there were things that were right too. Everything was wrong except for his wife and daughter.

He remembered a conversation he'd once had with the cleaning lady, the girl as he called her, Agnieszka, who'd failed to turn up that morning without letting them know.

"What about you, do you get scared sometimes?" he'd said. "Is there anything you're scared of?"

"No, I'm not scared of anything. Nothing gets the better of me."

"Come on," the man said. "You must be scared sometimes."

"Yes," she said. "I am scared sometimes."

"You see? And I'm scared too," the man said.

"Yes, yes." The young Polish woman laughed. "Absolutely."

When the girl woke up the following day the boy wasn't there. Nobody was there. She took a bath. The boy didn't come back. She waited. She turned on a large television and watched cartoons. By six o'clock there was still nobody there. She switched off the television and walked through the apartment. She looked for a telephone but couldn't find one.

She left and arrived half an hour early for work at the pub, because she hoped the boy would be waiting for her, but he wasn't there.

"What now?" the girl's mother's friend said.

"Indeed, what now?" the mother said. It was late morning. "I don't know."

Cigarettes. Old newspapers. The view out of the window.

Once, years ago, they'd thought about taking a photograph every hour, a photo of the west-facing view out of the window every hour, showing everything changing before their eyes, the wall vanishing before their eyes, but it wasn't an especially original idea and they didn't discuss it again. The girl's mother remembered this, perhaps her friend didn't. What about taking a photo at the window every hour from now? the girl's mother thought, but she kept it to herself.

The boy looked for Icke. He took the U-Bahn to Kreuzberg. He'd been to Kreuzberg with Icke, to Wrangelkiez and Görlitzer Park. Last summer they'd bought dope in Görlitzer Park. They'd drunk beer at lunchtime and then lain in the sun.

Now, in the snow, the park was empty. The boy scampered through Kreuzberg, as if he were being chased, but there was nothing urging him on. He knew he wouldn't find Icke.

In Oranienstrasse he saw the Chilean on the other side of the road. The Chilean was standing outside a Turkish barber's, talking to another man. He saw the boy. He gave him a friendly wave and then made a gesture as if aiming a rifle and shooting at him.

"Haven't you got a home? You need to go home."

The Chilean laughed.

"Children don't belong on the street! Didn't I tell you about the wolf? You'd better look out for your friend or the wolf will come and gobble her up. See you!"

The Chilean laughed again and went on talking to the man.

The boy kept walking. It was only two in the afternoon. He

crossed the Landwehrkanal and found himself standing outside the American Memorial Library.

He was cold and he didn't know what to do. He went into the library supposing that they wouldn't let him, but that's not what happened. Nobody stopped him.

Inside the library he wandered up and down the shelves, taking out books at random, flicking through them and putting them back. In the end he took out a picture book about the Sahara and sat at one of the tables.

An overweight man with long grey hair and a bushy beard was sitting opposite him, leafing through a book with photographs of steel sculptures. The boy cast a glance at the page the man had open in front of him. What he saw reminded him of a contorted, dead animal. The heavy man with the long grey hair noticed the boy peering over and said: "Venice."

The boy stayed in the library until half past five. Then he went to the U-Bahn and took a train to Alexanderplatz. Last summer he and Icke had begged outside the large department store on Alexanderplatz, to pay for their next beer.

From a telephone booth he called his mother.

"Hello, Mama."

"The T-33 is a good weapon, reliable, still reliable after all these years, but you can't shoot," the old man had said. "You've never held a gun before."

Charly took the money for the pistol out of his pocket and offered it to the man, but he wouldn't take it.

The man said he wouldn't give him the pistol.

"I'm not selling it to you."

"What?"

"I've changed my mind."

They were standing on the frozen field.

The man wrapped the pistol in the yellow cloth and turned back.

Charly followed him.

"I'll pay you whatever you want."

"I know," the man said. "I've had second thoughts."

Charly stayed where he was on the snowy field.

"I don't like it," the old man said. "I don't like it."

When he heard the voice of his mother on the telephone the boy thought of the village pond. He thought of the fence and the three broken concrete steps outside the front door of the little house he'd grown up in. He thought of the small window beside the door through which a little light trickled into the dark hallway.

From Alexanderplatz the boy took the tram that went up Prenzlauer Allee.

His mother had cried on the telephone. She'd cried because he was calling, because she'd been worried, "But Mama," and she'd cried because she hadn't heard anything from her husband for two days.

"But how come, isn't he in hospital?"

"No, he's not in hospital anymore, but I don't know where he is."

The boy walked across Helmholtzplatz. In spite of the snow and the darkness a few people were still standing around a concrete ping-pong table on Helmholtzplatz with bottles of beer. Icke wasn't among them. This is where the two of them had come, last summer.

He asked the men at the ping-pong table about Icke, and a man with a rash on his face said, "Icke. Yes, Icke. I don't know. No-one's seen him for a while. I think he's dead."

"Why do you think he's dead?" another of the drinkers said. "You can't just say he's dead."

"He's dead, I'm telling you."

"He isn't dead, he might have just gone away. You'd go away too if you could."

"Who says I'm even here?"

The boy wanted to go back to Icke's apartment one last time. He wanted to leave him a message in case he came back, even though he knew that all that was left of the house were the external walls and that Icke would never move back in. He'd lost him. The boy walked along one side of the square and was about to wander up Lychener Strasse.

The door to a pub was pushed open, then two men shoved a third, older man down the steps into the street. The man fell in the snow and lay before the boy. The man in the snow was the boy's father.

As on the previous day, the girl's father drove through the city looking for his daughter.

That evening he didn't return to the villa. The girl's father drove to his studio. He drove the large, old car into the courtyard of the former brewery, got out and pushed open the heavy iron door of his studio. He switched on his spotlights and heater and began to draw. He tried to draw his daughter's face, but couldn't. He drew and drew on large, cheap sheets of paper, which is what he'd always done, it was always the first and most difficult step, the foundation, but the drawings, the sketches didn't work and he knew why: he was scared. He tried to sketch his fear, outline it on paper, but at the same time he found this pathetic and then he realised he couldn't do anything, anything at all. In the middle of his empty studio he sat in an old armchair that his wife – his new wife – and he had found in the street. He sat there and had a drink. On the floor lay the abortive sheets of paper and in front of him the enormous sculpture he was working on, the steel skeleton of a sperm whale, life-size, a creation that was both delicate and extraordinarily heavy.

They hadn't poured the skeleton, he and his wife and his assistants had reproduced, changed and simplified it. A stranded animal in danger of collapsing under its own weight.

The fridge was empty. Her friend wasn't there. The girl's mother went shopping. She walked down the steps of the apartment block. Not many of the people from her time still lived in the building. A dentist from the West had rocked up after the wall came down and now the property belonged to him. The dentist tried to raise the rents, but it proved more difficult than he'd thought. But when someone moved out or was evicted or died, their apartments were renovated, new floors were laid, new kitchens and windows installed, and then the rents shot up. The old tenants in the block called the dentist "a twat" and the new tenants called him Dr Nolte.

The girl's mother walked up Schwedter Strasse to the cheap supermarket at the end of the road. She went up and down the supermarket aisles, she was hungry. She bought sliced cheese and cooked ham in plastic packets, and tinned tuna and herring salad, and all the time she thought: This is garbage.

She wondered how much of what she was buying had anything to do with fish, she thought that the fish in the packaging wasn't fish anymore, but a machine, or part of a machine or part of a factory, and then she had the idea for a sculpture or an object where a fish turns into a machine, and all of a sudden she understood what she'd vaguely made out in the darkness of the studio while talking in the courtyard to her ex-husband, the girl's father: the steel skeleton of an animal, a whale.

He'd had a similar idea, bones becoming metal, but he'd got there first or, she wondered, had she only thought of it because she'd seen the sculpture without realising what she had seen? She bought two bottles of champagne, because at Aldi you buy cheap champagne, that's what they used to do, she and her husband.

"It's the only thing worth buying there," her husband used to say.

The girl's mother bought bread and wine, but then thought there was nothing to celebrate, nothing at all, so why was she buying champagne, or was her daughter's disappearance a reason to celebrate? No, it wasn't, she thought. The girl's mother felt sick momentarily, warm saliva, but all the same she left the two bottles in her shopping trolley. She talked aloud to herself without noticing, twice she said: "Shit, shit!"

There's always something to celebrate, the girl's father used to say.

"Hello, young lady," the man at the checkout said, a man of her age, mid- to late forties, maybe the branch manager, she thought. Young lady, that's what they say in Berlin, that's how people address you. Young lady and young man, no matter how old you are. She smiled, she hadn't heard that in ages.

Her eyes met those of the man at the checkout, the man looked at her expectantly and then she realised she recognised his face, but didn't know where from. She racked her brains for a name and a place for the face. The man smiled.

"At Karina's, Christburger Strasse, first in her apartment and then up on the roof, New Year's Eve, there was sparkling wine. Can't be more than thirty years ago."

For a few seconds the girl's mother said nothing, then she said: "Bilbao."

A map of the world had hung in the hall of the apartment.

"I want to go to Bilbao. I want to go to Marrakesh, to Lampedusa, I want to go to Toulouse and I want to go to Chania," that's what the man – hardly more than a boy back then – had kept saying at the party in Christburger Strasse, Prenzlauer Berg, Berlin, capital of the German Democratic Republic.

Bilbao, Marrakesh, Toulouse . . .

"Could be a poem," she'd said at the time.

"It *is* a poem," he'd said.

They hadn't known each other, and they never saw each other again afterwards.

Back then they believed the border would never come down. They were in their early twenties and they'd thought they would never get out of the G.D.R.

She would have loved to see the wolf itself, just once. Instead she talked to people who'd seen it, she talked to a kiosk owner, she talked to one of the commuters who'd seen the wolf from a train, and she talked to a woman from Vorkuta called Olga.

These were people who'd called the newspaper wanting to tell their stories, wanting to say how they'd seen the wolf, and so the newspaper had sent the woman to meet them.

Olga, the woman from Vorkuta, said she'd been in Weissensee in the morning, or between Weissensee and Marzahn, and then she'd seen the wolf on the edge of a car park.

"In Vorkuta we say that the stork brings the children, but the wolf takes them away, and then one morning I actually see a wolf, a wolf, do you hear me? I almost died of fright, that's impossible, a wolf on the streets of Berlin, but I really saw it and then thought of Vladik and Mila."

"Who's Vladik," the Turkish woman said as she jotted down the names, now she had a notebook and a dictaphone, "and who's Mila?"

Vladik was only six weeks old and his mother, Milena, or

Mila, had fallen very sick after the child's birth, but the woman from Vorkuta wouldn't say what was wrong with the child's mother, she just hinted vaguely.

"She's so sick she can't even hold a spoon."

Olga looked after the family who, like her, were from Russia, the father couldn't look after them because he had to work, he'd just found work as a heating engineer. That winter, everyone's heating was breaking down and the husband of the sick woman with the new-born baby had to work day and night. The woman was alone with the child and Olga helped her.

"The stork brings the children, but the wolf takes them away, I thought, and then I thought, I hope nothing's happened to Vladik, I hope nothing's happened to the baby."

The woman said she ran to the family's apartment.

"I've never run so fast in all my life, never, up all those stairs, it wasn't far, they live in Weissensee too, and there's a brothel on the floor below, I really think there is, and then I opened the door – I've got a key – and inside the apartment it was deathly quiet. Deathly quiet."

The woman from Vorkuta paused.

"Do you know how cold it gets in Vorkuta in winter? Minus forty degrees. Minus forty. In winter the wolves would come close to our houses. Really close. So close."

The woman was holding up her hand with thumb and forefinger pressed together.

"Deathly quiet, it was. And then . . ."

She looked the young Turkish woman in the eye and paused again.

"And then I see the child on the floor. Vladik is lying on the floor and Mila is standing on the balcony. So I picked up the child and said to Mila, 'Milotshka, come back in, it's cold outside, what are you doing out there,' and . . . well, it was a miracle," said the woman from Vorkuta, at the edge of the Urals in Russia.

"A miracle. You see, the wolf hadn't taken the baby away, it had saved it. And the mother too."

"Yes, that must have been a miracle," said the Turkish woman, who didn't believe a word of what she'd heard and yet wrote the story a few hours later, because a story is a story, and then she wrote the story of the man who'd seen the wolf by the bins behind a supermarket, and the story of a child in the Bornholm allotments.

The boy didn't recognise his father straightaway. The boy's father was completely drunk. His face was smeared with blood, his clothes wet. Maybe he'd spilled a beer, maybe someone had poured a beer over him, maybe he'd peed his pants. He lay helpless on his back in the snow. He didn't try to get up. The man's thin, grey hair stuck to his blood-smeared face. The boy and his father looked at each other without speaking. They had the same flattish face, the same large, angular head.

The last time the boy had seen his father was just over two weeks ago, before the boy's father had got paralytic and wandered onto the railway tracks in Beeskow. The boy wasn't sure if his father recognised him. He just looked at him, then walked on.

"Micha," the boy's father called after him. "Micha, help me, I can't manage on my own."

The man was slurring his speech. The boy continued on his way.

"Where's the girl?" the man called out. "I went looking for you. I followed your tracks. I walked through the entire forest. And then I found a dead body."

The boy stopped and went back.

The boy's father could barely stand. The boy supported him as best he could, but they made slow progress. The boy's father stank.

"Where are we going?" the man said. He stumbled twice, the boy wasn't always able to support the man's weight.

"Have you heard about the wolf, Micha, have you heard about it?"

They walked down Schönhauser Allee until they came to the pub. The girl was standing behind the bar. There weren't many people in the pub. The boy's father gripped tight onto the bar.

"He was lying in the street," the boy said.

"Where were you?" the girl asked.

"I went looking for Icke."

"And?"

"I didn't find him."

She looked at him.

"What now?"

The boy's father started muttering to himself.

"You've got to get him out of here," she said.

"Yes," he said. "I'm going to take him back."

"Where?" she said.

"Home," he said.

"You're going back?"

"I'm taking him back. He'll fall in the snow and won't get up. He'll die."

"He's dying anyway," the girl said.

"Where would you go?" she'd asked him the day before, in the enormous apartment they used to live in together. "In this cold? I'd go to a café. A bar that never closes."

"And then? I know where I'd go," she'd said after that. "To the cinema or a library."

They used to call the apartment the paper palace and the paper palace stood in a forest of stone, or in a fossilised forest. The girl's father stood at the window, looking out at the river, the river beyond which the border once ran. They used to call the river the "divide", the "crack", the "slit", the "gash" and the "cunt", and from this came the next name, the name for the wall that surrounded West Berlin, or Berlin (West), like a ring. In the paper palace they began by calling it the "ring", which became the "French letter" or "rubber johnny" and finally just "rubber". As a consequence, sometimes West Berlin wasn't the "forest of stone", but the "rubber cell" or "padded cell" or even the "reservoir", and that became the "reservation".

"Take me to my brother," the boy's father said when they were back out on the street outside the black pub where the girl worked.

"I'm not going back home."

They walked a little way down the street. The boy supported his father. The boy's father said again: "I'm not going back." He fell.

The boy helped him up.

"I'm not going back!" The boy's father raised his voice. He yelled. He yanked himself free and walked, or staggered, into the middle of the road.

The boy went after him. He hadn't seen or heard the car.

He flew over the car's windscreen and ended up lying on the road.

"I'm not going back!" the man shouted from the other side of the road. Then he shouted: "Where are you?"

He couldn't see the boy.

The boy stood up again immediately, or stood up as quickly as he could. The boy had rolled over the car and hit the tarmac, but he got up again straightaway. He looked down at himself, he moved his legs, arms and head – and then his knees gave way and he felt sick. He sat on the pavement. He wanted to say something, call out something, but he couldn't speak.

They took him to hospital, to the Charité, casualty department, Luisenstrasse, Berlin Mitte.

Driving in the car had been a young couple, he was a tax expert and she worked in accounts. He'd been behind the wheel, they were on their way to her parents, a birthday, much too late. The boy had appeared in the road as if from nowhere.

They didn't wait for an ambulance, they put the boy on the back seat and drove off. I'm not in any pain, the boy wanted to say, but still he couldn't speak. He felt cold. His head was bleeding, he hadn't noticed at first. The car radio was on.

"Are you alright," the woman kept asking, over and over again, "are you alright?"

It was First Aid, they said later. He was lying on the road.

In the hospital they put him in a dark room with four beds, high up above the city, under observation, as it was called. From the window you could see trains running and a river in the night. The moon was shining.

His hip hurt, ribs, shoulder, neck, the cut they'd sewn up with four stitches.

"You were lucky," the assistant doctor on night duty had said, but the boy, who'd regained his speech, talked only of his father and a girl, where was his father, where was the girl, Elisabeth?

They put him on a drip and then the boy slept through the night and the next day and through most of the following night.

He ate too much, and often. He could also go for long periods without eating, a whole day or even longer, he could go to sleep hungry and wake up hungry and keep going, as in the times when there had been something to keep going for, but once he'd started eating, especially when he sat down at a dining table, at the table of a former colleague, for example, a big meeting, old work colleagues, old friends, he couldn't stop, and when the table had been cleared he kept eating and people made jokes at his expense, and he too made jokes at his own expense and then at some point he would watch the plate being taken into the kitchen. He drank a lot, but not as much as his brother, the poor sod.

Years ago he'd left the village. He'd learned to be an electrician and found work in a Berlin theatre, he became a lighting technician. He lived alone on Dunckerstrasse, Prenzlauer Berg, Berlin. Long hair. No girlfriend. Married once and now divorced.

On the ground floor of his block there had once been a pub, but that had closed ages ago and now a children's clothes shop had opened up there.

He was a good chess player.

He knew everything better, he'd always been the one who knew everything better, who'd read everything, who was ready to change everything and in whose life nothing changes. The people in the pub liked him, or at least they put up with him even though he always had to have the last word, and that's why at the end of nights in the pub it had always been so quiet.

The people at work didn't like him, they never had. In the canteen the lighting technicians and stagehands sat at different tables, and at another table sat the artists, the directors, the actors. Separate worlds. The actors stayed for a few years, the directors changed, some were nice, some screamed their heads off, and all of them were scared, he could see it, for he saw everything, he knew everything, even if nobody asked him.

He'd been pleased when his brother turned up. They'd drunk together. They'd drunk a lot, then they'd gone out to a kiosk that night and when they woke up the following morning it went on, they kept drinking, it was a special day after all, and then his brother had disappeared just as he was explaining something to someone in a pub. He'd gone home. His brother didn't come back after him. The man thought his brother had gone home. Back to the village. That was nice. Until next time.

The boy's father stood on the other side of the street, shouting: "I'm not going back." Then he shouted: "Where are you?" And when he couldn't see the boy anymore, he left.

Or rather, he staggered as he went, which annoyed him, so he stood up straight, took a deep breath and tried to regain control of his balance. He wanted to go to his brother's apartment in Dunckerstrasse, but he headed for the television tower on Alexanderplatz.

As the minutes passed he became increasingly aware of his mistake and then the mistake already had a solution, which he forgot the moment it entered his head, and there he was again, the doctor in the cowboy boots, and there was the dead man in the forest, and then the man was standing at some pedestrian lights on Münzstrasse, where he fell, slumped against the lights. This irritated him, and with the irritation he felt better, he saw the tower before him, his son's appearance seemed to him as natural as his disappearance, and already he'd stopped thinking about it, he'd think about it tomorrow, he decided, because there was no hurry, and then he stood on Alexanderplatz in the darkness, in front of the bright windows of the department store, he looked at the light, he saw the doors of the department store open and close, he saw all the people and he tried to stick to a plan that had never existed, and now he realised that, yet at the same time he didn't because the next plan was already there, and the one after that. Everything was so dark and everything so light.

A telephone. A tram. Something to drink.

He crawled. He crawled along the windows of the large department store in the slush, and that was part of a plan which would work, just as the plan on the railway tracks would have worked if they hadn't stopped him, and now, now all he had to do was find the entrance to the department store, which had been just in front of him, had it not?

The security man at the entrance to the department store watched the crawling man try to get to his feet by a closed glass door, and saw how the crawling man failed to understand the transparent obstacle. Now the man's forehead was leaning against the glass of the door, staring in at the light, apparently seeing nothing or at least not making anything out, and breathing through his open mouth. Then the man turned around, still leaning against the door, still trying to support himself with the glass door, eventually sliding down with his back to it. He sat doubled over and didn't move again after that. A man and woman were playing bagpipes. A few metres away on the square, someone had strapped a grill to their belly and was selling sausages.

It was late at night when the girl's father came back, his wife had been waiting for him, but when finally he returned they didn't talk much.

Unable to sleep, he turned on the television and watched a war film, which in its grisly realism was like nothing he'd ever seen before, and after that he watched another film, a comedy with actors he knew vaguely from years back, or had known once, before they were on television or in the cinema.

Then he switched off the television, or his wife switched it off, and he stared at the ceiling. It occurred to him that these two films put into question everything he'd ever thought meaningful. In the end he found himself asking: what was meaningful, or did anything at all have meaning? To his mind, these two films signified the end of all meaning, and he wondered what the meaning was of reproducing a whale skeleton out of steel, and the answer he came up with was that it had no meaning, except perhaps that he was creating and doing something different from what other people were creating and doing. War films and comedies.

He thought of how he and his daughter's mother had bought

the schoolhouse in the village, at the time they'd created something, or at least tried to, and the creation had nothing to do with war films or comedies, but the creation hadn't worked. Then he waited in the dark for the telephone to ring, but it didn't.

He thought of his father, who'd died as a result of a war wound, a piece of shrapnel that migrated through his body, that nobody had been able to remove.

When the Chilean showed up in the pub a few hours later he asked where the boy was. The girl shrugged.

"He must have gone away."

"Did you have an argument? I don't like arguments!"

"No," the girl said, "we didn't argue."

The girl hoped that the boy would come back that night, but he didn't.

The Chilean stood behind the bar and briefly put his arm around her waist.

As on previous nights, after work they walked in the morning half-light to the basement apartment. He'd brought along a bottle of tequila and the girl was slightly drunk. She took a couple of puffs of the joint the waitress handed around.

Hours later she woke up in the Chilean's bed, feverish and headachey. Someone had taken her clothes off.

She writes the story of the kiosk owner who saw the wolf outside Marzahn but couldn't photograph it.

She writes the story of the man in the kebab shop, whose uncle had come back from the mountains with a dead wolf over his shoulder.

An old couple sits on a sofa on the seventh floor of a mansion block in Behmstrasse. They're happy to be here, they came years ago from Transylvania in Romania. They badmouth their neighbours, people from Syria, Ghana and Turkey.

"From Turkey?" the young woman says. "I bet they're nice people."

The couple had been looking out of the window, and there it was, a wolf, a wolf on the edge of the sports pitch.

"Are you sure?" the trainee asks. "It could also have been a dog."

A woman talks about a miracle, about a Russian woman standing on a balcony who was about to jump.

The young Turkish woman travels out to Zehlendorf, where she hears a story from a man who'd only heard it himself, it had happened in Silesia long before the war. A story of farmsteads, four-horse carriages and furs. She takes notes and looks it all up later in the encyclopaedia.

On the telephone she makes enquiries about the hunter who discovered the first wolf tracks, in Vierlinden bei Seelow.

She's got some ideas, she finds the picture editor who bought the photo off Agnieszka, the photo of the wolf by the side of the motorway, which Tomasz took, then she writes the story, another wolf story.

"It was one of those moments you never forget," the editor says. "That day our cleaning lady came, well, the girl or young woman who cleans for us and sometimes looks after the children, and she said, 'You work for a newspaper, don't you? I have to show you something.' I thought, what's this going to be? And then she showed me the picture her boyfriend had taken the night before, on the motorway, I couldn't believe it at first, the young Polish man had taken the picture and it went around the world, yes, really, all around the world, and I've been meaning to give her the money, but I haven't seen her since, she hasn't come, perhaps she's unwell."

And so she gave the trainee of Turkish origin the task of searching for the Polish girl and her boyfriend, another wolf story, the woman gave her the mobile number, but the Polish cleaning lady didn't answer her phone and there was no address.

The Chilean came home and kissed her on the lips. The girl looked for her things and left the apartment. She found her way back to Lychener Strasse, she would go back to Icke's apartment, she thought perhaps the boy would be there. Perhaps he was waiting there.

She had a temperature.

She felt her way upwards in the darkness of the stairwell, step by step, to the fourth floor, no light anywhere. Nobody was there.

The entire city in uproar. The newspapers, the headlines. The local television. The news going across the globe. The wolf of Berlin. People of the world, look at this city, see how it has changed. This wolf is a Berliner.

At the top end of Mauerpark is a camera team, its lenses aimed into the distance, the hollow, the passing trains, not far from the cut-price supermarket Aldi.

This is where the wolf was last spotted. Berlin, the green city, now white with snow, or grey, because it hasn't snowed in two days.

"When the sun comes," Charly said. "Jacky, when the March sun comes it'll all be over."

"What will be over, Charly? I don't understand, what will be over when the March sun comes?"

"When the March sun comes the snow will disappear."

"And then? What's so bad about the snow disappearing, Charly? I'm glad when the snow goes, it's about time."

"When the snow disappears, Jacky, no-one will find the wolf. It'll be gone."

Jacky, Jacqueline really, convenience store owner, knew

that she sometimes got the days of the week mixed up because she worked every day and because every day was the same, and she knew that she and Charly would never have children. She knew that Charly didn't want children, let's think the whole thing through properly, let's think it all through properly from start to finish:

It would mean having to give up everything, the shop and Charly and the past few years, everything ruined, having to look for a new husband, and how would it all work out, when would she tell him? Nobody's humiliated you.

"What are you thinking about, Charly? You look so strange, you've got such a strange expression."

Charly was thinking about the man who'd refused to sell him the pistol. He thought of the blanket of snow on the old sewage farm.

Charly imagined himself going down into the railway trench with a rifle over his shoulder. It would be better if there were more men with him, beaters and hounds, he'd read about this in a book a long time ago, Tolstoy.

"Have you ever read any Tolstoy, Jacky?"

"No, Charly."

"Don't you ever read, Jacky?"

"I do read. You know I do."

Charly knew what Jacky read.

"The rubbish needs putting out," Jacky said. Change of subject.

"Exactly," Charly said. No inclination.

Charly imagined climbing down into the railway trench, up at Mauerpark, with the beaters, or he imagined hunting the wolf alone, laying out bait and setting traps, he imagined lying in wait for the wolf at dawn, then shooting it in the railway trench, but sometimes he shifted the setting to Friedrichshain, to the top of the hill in the park, at the viewing point. He dreamed of the wolf.

He dreamed that he shot the wolf dead.

"Well, little one, would you like to warm yourself up?" the old lady said. "Come on in."

The heat and stench inside the apartment were unbearable.

"We've still got coal," the old lady said, "the one thing we've still got is coal. That's a very red face you've got. What would you like to drink? Get her something to drink," she called out.

There was snow in the cup that the old man put down in front of the girl.

"Our dog has gone, have you seen a dog out there?"

"I haven't seen any dog," the girl said.

"Have you got a temperature?" the old lady asked. "You look as if you've got a temperature, don't you want to go home?"

"I'm looking for my friend," she said. And then she said: "Or Icke. There used to be someone here called Icke who lived on the fourth floor."

"A girl used to live on the fourth floor, Maria, she was called, she got thinner and thinner and then one day she was gone. I think she vanished into thin air."

She made a gesture.

"Gone. And one day she was simply gone."

The old man sat at the small table in the hallway.

"You've got to watch out," he said. "You've got to watch out."

"You'd be better off watching out for yourself," the old lady said.

A train passed by outside, right beside the house, in the railway trench.

A sheet of burning paper fell onto the street in front of the girl.

"You're back," the woman on the balcony said. "Come on up."

In the woman's apartment it smelled of sandalwood and incense. Lots of candles were burning. The girl had the shivers. The woman gave her a tea, she had nothing else in the house for a temperature, no aspirin, no ibuprofen. She didn't believe in tablets.

The girl lay under a blanket on the sofa, gazing at the candles.

"How old are you?" the woman asked, but the girl didn't reply. "Where's your friend?"

"I don't know," the girl said.

"Do you know what?" the woman said. "I think I saw the wolf."

"Really?"

Tomasz and Agnieszka were in their apartment in Neu-kölln. Since coming back from the hospital they'd barely exchanged a word. His head was bandaged. He'd come into the apartment and fallen asleep straightaway, but then kept waking up. His head hurt.

She cancelled work and stayed in the apartment. She called Janina and then she called Krzysztof, Janina's boyfriend. Krzysztof and Janina were from Poland, like them, she worked as a sales assistant and he worked in a garage.

She called Marek and said that Tomasz wouldn't be able to come to work that week because he was ill. A fall. A hole in his head.

"He's got a hole in his head as it is. But wish him a speedy recovery."

Agnieszka prayed. She changed the bedclothes.

For the next few days they didn't leave the apartment. Tomasz wanted to go back to Poland, but he didn't say so. The television was on. Tomasz had a lot to say to her, in his head he said many things, as he did when he was in Poland or on the building site, but his head hurt and he couldn't say what he wanted to say, it was as if his thoughts couldn't express themselves in words, even though they were so close.

They didn't touch each other.

They took the car to the garage and Krzysztof fitted it with a new window.

Seeing the bandage on Tomasz's head, Krzysztof asked: "What happened?"

"Nothing," Tomasz said.

The rifle was leaning against the wall in the corner of the room.

Tomasz wanted to take the bullets out of the barrel, but she screamed at him not to touch the rifle.

Agnieszka was scared of the rifle.

The rifle had to go, but she didn't know what to do with it. She thought about just throwing it away, but she was worried that someone might find it, perhaps a child.

Two days after the rifle went off in the car she went back to work. She took Tomasz with her.

They drove to Prenzlauer Berg, where she should have cleaned the day before, where she cleaned every Monday and Friday. For the woman she'd given the photograph to a few days earlier, but the woman wasn't there.

They found a parking space right outside the entrance to the old apartment building on Kollwitzplatz. Agnieszka had her own key. Agnieszka unlocked the front door. Tomasz stayed in the open doorway. Then she went back to the car and waited. To the left of the entrance was a kiosk with late-night opening. She waited until she couldn't see anyone on the pavement, then grabbed the rifle from the car and ran inside the house. They let the large door close behind them. Agnieszka went to the rear courtyard of the apartment building, threw the rifle into one of the large black dustbins and ran back into the hallway. They were rid of the rifle. Tomasz smiled.

They went into the apartment – nobody there, as was often the case. On the table were a few banknotes and a message for Agnieszka.

In case you come . . .
Everything O.K.?

Agnieszka worked for several hours while Tomasz sat on the sofa. He made the occasional comment about the people's taste in interiors. Light-green sofa. Funny colour.

"Yes, my sweetheart, funny colour."

Black-and-white photographs on the wall, cut out of newspapers but framed. A bloody pair of spectacles and a half-empty glass. A flag above Berlin in ruins. A bridge. The wolf by the road sign.

When Agnieszka had finished she locked the door to the apartment from the outside, three locks, and took down the rubbish bag she'd put in the hallway. In the courtyard she opened the large black bin she had tossed the rifle into. The rifle was no longer there.

That evening Tomasz sat in the open-plan office, watching Agnieszka work. He had a headache and wasn't really able to help her.

Sitting at one of the desks in the huge office, in the light of the fluorescent lamps, he watched her vacuum the blue carpet in her grey tracksuit bottoms and large white T-shirt, and said nothing.

The girl's mother stood again at the window in the apartment above the Gleimtunnel, as she had done for most of the day before, and finally she told her friend that they really ought to take a photo every hour, of her, but her friend didn't take any photos.

She'd called the police, the station at the corner of Invalidenstrasse and Brunnenstrasse, and received an unfriendly response: It's the weekend, no-one here, call back next week. Then she'd driven there, but the response was no better than on the telephone. She drove back to Schwedter Strasse and stood beside the fence of the goat enclosure. "I'm driving home," she said.

The girl's mother had smoked, even though that was frowned upon inside the zoo.

"The goats are called Katinka and Natascha," her friend said. "Let's go out this evening," her friend said. "Drive home tomorrow."

In the afternoon Jacky found the rifle behind the counter. She stood there by the cigarette section holding the rifle with both hands, the muzzle pointing to the ceiling. Charly stood with his back to her, rearranging the magazines on the shelf, photographic magazines, sports magazines, house and garden, kitchen, art, hunting, tattoos, everything.

"Where did you get this, Charly?"

"What, Jacky, where did I get what?"

"This, where did you get this, this rifle?"

He turned to her.

"I found it in the bin."

"Where?"

She raised her voice.

"Where did you find it?"

"It was in the rubbish. Here, in the courtyard—"

"Then take it straight back."

She was about to lose her temper.

"Jacky, somebody put it there for me, nobody chucks a rifle away in the rubbish."

"Take it back! Now!"

She was shouting now. He'd never heard her shout before. She'd never shouted at him.

"Now!"

"Too loud, Jacky, you're shouting—"

"What are you going to do with it now, what are you planning to do with it now?"

"What am I going to do with it?"

He was beginning to yell himself.

"You don't have to say everything three times, Jacky—"

"What, Charly, what are you going to do with it now, that's what I want to know, what are you going to do with it?"

Charly opened his eyes wide – a habit, a nervous tic.

"I . . . it humiliated me, it humiliated *us*—"

"It didn't humiliate you, nobody's humiliated you, but now you're thinking of marching off," she said, still at the top of her voice, "marching off with that rifle over your shoulder, and lying in wait?"

As she said "lying in wait" she pulled a face and opened her eyes wide, just as he so often did. The walls painted black, red and gold. The wall full of newspapers. The two fridges, beer, water, coke, wine, sparkling wine.

"You haven't understood, Jacky, don't you understand that we, *we* are the eyes?"

Jacky began to cry, her grip still tight on the rifle.

"We're not the eyes, Charly, we're just a shitty little shop selling lottery tickets."

Jacky cried.

He wanted to take the rifle from her and put it back under the counter.

"We are the eyes."

She wouldn't let go. She carried it to the door of the kiosk, past the lottery sign.

Charly followed her, they walked down the street, she in front with the rifle, he keeping a few metres' distance and turning around the whole time, the shop was still open. She walked past the hairdresser's and turned the corner. Charly stopped and went back.

"Put the radio on, Tomek," Agnieszka said, "I can't bear this silence."

Tomasz sat with his bandaged head at one of the white desks in the open-plan office on Rosa-Luxemburg-Platz and said, "There's no radio here, we've never heard a radio here."

"There must be one somewhere."

She was in pain. Cramps.

On some of the desks beside the telephones and screens stood framed photographs. In the kitchenette he found a small radio and turned it on. First there was music and then somebody was talking about the wolf.

"There it is again," Agnieszka said.

"Who?" said Tomasz, who barely understood a word of German.

"Your wolf, the wolf you saw."

"*My* wolf?"

"On the radio they're talking about the wolf you brought, it's your wolf, you brought it with you and now nobody knows where it's hiding."

"I know where he is," Tomasz said. "Or I know where I'd go looking for him."

Music.

She vacuumed the carpet of the open-plan office, the radio played music and he sat on the desk.

The cramps became more and more intense. She tried to breathe deeply and carry on, but then she said she would have to go home soon, she couldn't keep on working, it was too painful, and he didn't know what to say, he spoke to his mother, telling her all those things he couldn't say, also about the child that was another man's.

Agnieszka began to panic because of the pain, she told him to call Janina and then she said she had to go to hospital.

Tomasz was the first to see the blood on her grey tracksuit bottoms, he said "Agnieszka", and she looked at him.

In the end she was convulsing with pain on the floor and he sat beside her. The radio was still playing.

They went from pub to pub, and in some pubs they met old acquaintances. Haven't seen you in years. How are you? Fine. They started off in Kiez, near the Gleimtunnel, and then the girl's mother and her friend walked tipsily down Schönhauser Allee until they came to a pub painted completely black, and the woman asked, "What's this place called? I don't know it," and the friend said it must be called Orkus, at which the two of them in the street laughed so much that it almost hurt, and the girl's mother wiped away her tears, she hadn't laughed so much in ages, not in a long, long time, but she wondered what, in fact, was so funny. They went into the pub, behind the bar stood a woman and a dark-haired man.

"My, you look like you're in a bad mood," the girl's mother said to the man she had never seen before, and he said: "One of my barmaids has done a runner."

"There are worse things in life," the red-headed woman said.

A woman beside them turned to her, she was a friend from the old days, an actress she used to know well, when she was in her mid- to late twenties.

"I know that voice," the actress said, "what are you doing

here, what a coincidence, we haven't seen each other in years."

The actress had been highly successful as a young woman, but then it went quiet, and these days she was looking for work like anyone else, keeping her head above water, as she put it. The three of them stayed at the bar and talked and talked. They had a lot of catching up to do, they laughed a lot, all three of them were quick-witted and funny and it was almost like the old days, and then the girl's mother told her old friends that she'd hit her daughter, and the actress had an explanation for this, a justification, it was all about mirroring, playing out the unspoken aggression of your counterpart.

"I'm not going back," the girl's mother said. She said, "He buried me alive because he always knew I'd be a threat to him. He destroyed me."

They drank beer and schnapps and got into conversation with the man behind the counter. He said he came from Chile and the women said, "We don't believe a word of it, you're from Romania, you're Romanian," and the Chilean laughed and said: "Yes, maybe I am, but don't tell anyone."

"Here's to the Danube," the girl's mother said. "To Romania and Chile."

"To the blue Danube," the friend said. "To Chile on the blue Danube."

"Do you know about colours?" the Chilean said.

"Yes, I do. Or at least I used to."

Then the women went on talking without the Chilean, and the Chilean glanced over at them only occasionally.

When they arrived home in the early hours, tired and drunk, at Mauerpark beyond the Gleimtunnel, in the old apartment with its view across the railway trench, they heard the wolf howling in the distance.

The boy dreamed of Icke. In his dream Icke was living in a hole underground, but the hole was made out of metal, and then the boy dreamed of his father. He woke up, fell asleep again, then woke up and fell asleep again. This is how he spent a night and a day and another night.

When he awoke on his second night in hospital the moon through the window stood high above the city, above the river and the railway tracks.

Then he dreamed again, he dreamed of the woods, and when he awoke he thought for a split second that he was still with the girl in the little chapel in the forest cemetery, but then through the window the boy saw the river and the tracks and he tried to get up. It was around three o'clock in the morning.

Although he felt pain he was able to move. A drip had been connected to the back of his hand. He pulled out the needle, blood.

The boy got up. It hurt, as if something inside him had torn. He was able to walk. The boy looked for his clothes and found them in a cupboard.

In the bed beside him lay an old man, asleep.

He went into the corridor on the ward. There was no-one to be seen, all was quiet, everyone asleep. He walked down the long corridor. A door was open to a room in which a nurse sat with her back to him. She didn't turn around as he passed. She hadn't heard him, but the boy knew that she would hear the automatic ward door. At that moment someone at the end of the corridor rang the night bell. A light went on above the door.

The boy leaned against the wall. The nurse came out of the room. The boy left the ward.

On the way down the lift stopped once, and a doctor in a coat got in. The doctor said nothing.

The boy crossed the hospital lobby, a man in a uniform looked up as he walked past, and outside the hospital were two police officers sitting in a patrol car, but nobody spoke to the boy. He stood in the street, unsure of where to go, right or left. He went right and then right again. He was in pain and didn't know for certain where he was. He looked for the television tower to get his bearings, but he couldn't see it. He decided to keep going straight. He'd been given painkillers in the hospital and now, as he walked, they were beginning to wear off. His hip hurt, his entire left side, his neck vertebrae, his chest when he breathed and his head. The boy walked along Invaliden-strasse. The boy walked past the Natural History Museum, he'd wanted to go there with Icke in the summer, but they never did. "What do you want to go in there for?" Icke had said. "It's just dinosaur skeletons and dead frogs."

The boy moved slowly, but he did not stop. Having little breaks is more tiring than keeping going, his father had told him in the woods one day when they'd suddenly got caught in bad weather.

The boy didn't stop until he came to a park at the corner of Brunnenstrasse, with a police station opposite. He'd almost run out of breath outside the police station, but then he managed to make it across the street and into the park.

Here children had played on sledges, he could see the tracks in the snow. He walked up the small slope until he fell. The boy flipped onto his back and looked up at the sky. It was a clear night, four o'clock in the morning, but the boy didn't have a watch. He sat up. He thought of the woods. He thought of the trailer, the fire, the dead man at the bottom of the ladder, he thought of the girl.

When at last he'd found his way back to the black-painted pub, the Chilean said: "She's not here."

"No idea where she is. Have a rest, you look tired," the Chilean said. "Has something happened? Have a drink, on me."

The wolf was standing ten metres away from him. Charly held the gun as the man in Hobrechtsfelde had shown him, with both hands.

Charly aimed at the wolf, but he knew that he wouldn't be able to keep the gun still. He knew that in all probability he wouldn't hit the wolf with the Tokarev from ten metres, and he knew that in the end the man hadn't sold him the Tokarev, but he *had* found the rifle, but now he had the pistol rather than the rifle – why? – and he was holding the pistol with both hands. The wolf wasn't moving, he stood before him just as he had in the driving snow that morning in Marzahn, when Charly was so frightened he was unable to move.

Charly didn't know what would happen if he missed, or what would happen if he hit the wolf without killing him. Both possible scenarios entered his mind at the same time and repeated themselves without anything happening, because he thought that nothing could happen if you weren't able to imagine it, let's think the whole thing through properly, and then he pulled the trigger, screaming, and Jacky tried to wake him.

"Charly, wake up."

He couldn't keep the pistol still.

"You don't know how to hold it," said the man on the icy field in Hobrechtsfelde, and Charly thought he'd aimed too low, but the wolf spun over and tried to get up again, even though he'd lost one of his front paws. Charly had shot off one of his paws. Charly fell to his knees. The animal was bleeding, but it didn't try to flee. The wolf got up again and stood on three legs.

A train appeared. Charly got up and walked away. He wanted to go closer to the wolf, and yet didn't, he walked away from him even though he wanted to go closer.

The woman talked a lot. The girl was lying on the sofa, wrapped in two blankets. One minute the girl was hot, the next she was cold. The woman sat on the floor, her back up against the sofa. She talked about religions and gods, about Indian gods and other gods, she talked about her parents, especially her mother who'd just died and whose diaries she'd burned, one after the other, on the balcony. The woman talked and talked, it was nice having someone in the house to talk to, she'd been on her own for a long time. She talked about her friends all over the world, in England, in Sweden, in the U.S.A. She talked about her master in India – she actually called him master – who had predicted that he would leave his body in a year. She said that men like him really knew when it was time to go. The master was a holy man and the woman showed her photographs of him. Music was playing, Indian music. The girl was half asleep and half awake. She hardly moved. She listened to the woman and gazed at the candles. Sometimes the woman's face appeared before her, a blonde woman with large, clear eyes and deep wrinkles and sometimes the girl thought it was her own face.

"Somebody's hit you on the eye and the mouth," the woman said.

The girl thought of their journey through the woods and in her fever it seemed as if she could remember every step.

When the girl woke up the following morning and looked out of the window he was standing down below in the street.

The boy was standing in a patch of sunlight in front of the house, in front of Icke's house.

She waved to him, but he didn't see her. The window was jammed, she couldn't open it.

She got dressed. She couldn't say goodbye or thank you, because the woman, Nadine, wasn't at home.

The girl pulled the door shut behind her and went down the stairs, three floors.

The boy was standing in the patch of sunlight at the end of Lychener Strasse. He looked pale. He smiled as she came out of the building.

For years there had been no linesmen on the S-Bahn. The function had died out, but now, in this long and cold winter, a number of men were sent out onto the tracks. As trains ran continually, save for a few hours in the night, and at three-minute intervals at peak times, it was seriously dangerous work, and nobody went out alone.

Between half past one and four o'clock in the morning the men checked the tunnels and the stations that were underground, and after sunrise they patrolled the sections above ground. They checked the bridges, the track bed, the points.

The men wore fluorescent orange overalls and yellow reflective coats. They wore helmets, work gloves and heavy-duty boots. When the trains ferrying commuters passed them in the morning light they stood still. Sometimes they looked up at the trains, waved to the drivers even though they didn't know them, letting tired faces at the windows roll past, and sometimes they didn't look, they just let the yellow trains go on their way. The men went mostly in pairs. One of these men was Icke. Icke walked in the trench of the ring railway, he had the sun on his back, and at one point he turned to look up at the house in which he'd once lived, until the day when a group of Polish construction workers had begun to gut the building. He stopped, turned around and looked up at the apartment. The house was covered in scaffolding and tarpaulin, which flapped in the wind. The windows had been knocked out. The house looked like a ruin.

Icke tried to remember how long he'd lived there, but he got his months mixed up and sometimes his years too. Up in that apartment he'd waited for the woman the apartment had belonged to. Once in summer a friend had visited him for two weeks, a friend from his village, younger than him, but a friend, one of the few he'd had there, but he couldn't remember his friend's name. The woman had given him the keys to the apartment, but then she'd disappeared and she never came back. He had almost gone mad.

A whistle, a few steps back, the train passed. Micha. That was his name, Icke thought, or was the boy called Mike? Micha.

He was working with a Vietnamese man who had come to the G.D.R. in the early eighties. The Vietnamese man was called Vinh.

"You know what, Icke?"

"What?"

"Blue's not a hair colour."

"Yes, it is. You can see it is."

"No. And what have you done to your neck?"

They kept going.

"Let me tell you something, Vinh."

"What?"

"There are tunnels all over the place here."

"Sure, tunnels all over the place, from the Nordbahnhof, Oranienburger Strasse, Potsdamer Platz."

"No, Vinh, no. Here – here, I mean here . . ."

Icke stamped his foot on the ground. "There are tunnels everywhere here. People dug tunnels here."

"In the war? Do you mean in the war?"

"Afterwards."

"Afterwards? When afterwards? What are you talking about?" Vinh laughed. "What are you talking about?"

"Beneath us the ground is hollow, Vinh. Hollow."

Icke knocked on the ground.

Vinh stopped. His boots were too big, everything was too big for him, his overalls, his coat.

"Hollow?"

"Hollow, Vinh, hollow. Cavities. Empty."

"If you say so."

If you say so – Vinh always said that.

"You always say that."

"What?"

"If you say so."

"Really?"

This got Vinh thinking. For a while he said nothing. They walked a few metres further along the tracks. A train in the opposite direction. One of the trains they glanced up at, both of them. A wave to the driver.

"Like in Vietnam, Icke. Did you know that?"

"What?"

"Everything hollow. Full of tunnels."

"No, I didn't."

Pause. Another train passed.

"I used to live up there."

"There?"

"There."

"There? In that house? Icke, you're crazy and that's why your hair grows blue."

The light from the morning sun, still low on the horizon. The yellow trains, the clouds, the planes in the sky heading for Berlin Tegel.

"That's the truth, you dwarf. Dwarves dig tunnels too, did you know that?"

"Dwarves, what are they, Icke?"

"Dwarves are giants."

They looked at the broad swathe of tracks in front of them, they saw the tracks that crossed from the east, west and north, and they knew it could be fatal to walk across this area.

They looked at each other and said nothing.

"Where are the others?" Vinh said after a while.

The trains in the distance, changing tracks, carriage after carriage.

At Gesundbrunnen station they had breakfast in an underground staff room that reeked of oil.

"Great air in here, Icke."

"Couldn't be better."

"Shame you're not allowed to smoke."

At the old iron bridge above Gartenstrasse they stood on a siding between a couple of juvenile birch trees. Vinh began to sing and Icke would have liked to sing along, but he didn't know the song.

Vinh had cigarettes, American cigarettes from China.

And then Icke saw the wolf, a haggard creature that stood for a moment on the tracks.

"Look at that, Vinh."

"What?"

"Look at that."

"What are you talking about?"

Vinh couldn't see the wolf at first, but then he did.

"What is it, Icke?"

"That's a wolf, Vinh."

A train arrived. It wasn't one of those trains they waved to, nor one of those they didn't look up at. Because they were on their break it was just another train passing through. When the train had gone the wolf was no longer there.

The sun came out.

That was the last time anyone saw the wolf, it was the day when the wolf's trail went cold.

People supposed that the wolf had been killed, hit by a train, or that it just died, maybe in a cavity or a tunnel, who knows? Some people believed the wolf had been shot dead, and others thought it had moved northwards, perhaps it had followed these tracks and left the city that way. Maybe it was in the woods to the north of Berlin, in the Schorfheide, but the hunters and foresters in these woods found no trace of a wolf, no prey torn to pieces.

The wolf had vanished.

ROLAND SCHIMMELPFENNIG, born in 1967, is Germany's most celebrated contemporary playwright. He was a journalist before studying to be a theatre director, and his plays have now been performed in more than forty countries, including America and Britain. Schimmelpfennig is the recipient of the highest play-writing award in Germany, the Else-Lasker-Schüler-Prize, to honour his entire oeuvre. *One Clear, Ice-Cold January Morning at the Beginning of the Twenty-First Century* is his first novel; it was shortlisted for the Leipzig Bookfair Prize in 2016. He lives in Berlin.

JAMIE BULLOCH is the translator of Timur Vermes' *Look Who's Back*, Birgit Vanderbeke's *The Mussel Feast*, which won him the Schlegel-Tieck Prize, *Kingdom of Twilight* by Steven Uhly, and novels by F. C. Delius, Jörg Fauser, Martin Suter, Katharina Hagena and Daniel Glattauer.